"Tasha, what's with you?" Sarah blinked in surprise. "You are just the most contrary person I've ever met!"

"Contrary to what?" Tasha raised her voice. "Contrary to who?"

"To everything and everyone!" Sarah said, feeling the anger rise in her voice. "I was looking forward to your coming. I thought we would be like sisters. I felt sympathy and friendship toward you. You just seem to feel hostility toward me."

Tasha glared at Sarah.

"And it's your mission to convince Kwame and Dave that I'm not so great, right?" Sarah stood with her hands on her hips. Tasha was saying things that just weren't true, and Sarah felt hurt.

"All I want to do is be Tasha Gordon," Tasha said. "And I think you're jealous of the attention the guys pay me, especially Dave. I haven't decided if I want him yet. When I make up my mind, I'll let you know."

Sarah whirled around and stormed out of Tasha's room. . . .

18 Pine St.

Sort of Sisters

Written by
Stacie Johnson

Created by
WALTER DEAN MYERS

A Seth Godin Production

BANTAM BOOKS
NEW YORK · TORONTO · LONDON · SYDNEY · AUCKLAND

RL 5, age 10 and up

SORT OF SISTERS
A Bantam Book / September 1992

*Special thanks to Judy Gitenstein, Betsy Gould, Amy Berkower, Fran Lebowitz,
Linda Lannon, Michael Cader, Monalisa DeGross, Helene Godin, and Lucy Wood.*

18 Pine St. is a trademark of Seth Godin Productions, Inc.

ISBN 0-553-29719-8

Published simultaneously in the United States and Canada

Bantam Books are published by Bantam Books, a division of Bantam
Doubleday Dell Publishing Group, Inc. Its trademark, consisting of the words
"Bantam Books" and the portrayal of a rooster, is Registered in U.S. Patent
and Trademark Office and in other countries. Marca Registrada. Bantam
Books, 666 Fifth Avenue, New York, New York 10103.

PRINTED IN THE UNITED STATES OF AMERICA

OPM 0 9 8 7 6 5 4 3 2 1

For Marjorie and Emily

18 Pine St.

There was a card shop at 8 Pine Street, and a shop that sold sewing supplies at 10 Pine that was only open in the afternoons and on Saturdays if it didn't rain. For some reason that no one seemed to know or care about, there was no 12, 14, or 16 Pine. The name of the pizzeria at 18 Pine Street had been Antonio's before Mr. and Mrs. Harris took it over. Mr. Harris had taken down Antonio's sign and just put up a sign announcing the address. By the time he got around to thinking of a name for the place, everybody was calling it 18 Pine.

The Crew at 18 Pine St.

Sarah Gordon is the heart and soul of the group. Sarah's pretty, with a great smile and a warm, caring attitude that makes her a terrific friend. Sarah's the reason that everyone shows up at 18 Pine St.

Tasha Gordon, tall, sexy, and smart, is Sarah's cousin. Since her parents died three years ago, Tasha has moved from relative to relative. Now she's living with Sarah and her family—maybe for good.

Cindy Phillips is Sarah's best friend. Cindy is petite, with dark, radiant skin and a cute nose. She wears her black hair in braids. Cindy's been Sarah's neighbor and friend since she moved from Jamaica when she was three.

Kwame Brown's only a sophomore, but that doesn't stop him from being part of the crew. Kwame's got a flattop haircut, dark glasses, and mischievous smile. As the smartest kid in the group, he's the one Jennifer turns to for help with her homework.

Jennifer Wilson is the poor little rich girl. Her parents are divorced, and all the charge cards and clothes in the world can't make up for it. Jennifer's tall and thin, with cocoa-colored skin and a body that's made for all those designer clothes she wears.

Dave Hunter is the boy next door. Sarah and Dave have been friends forever, but lately it seems like there might be something more. It doesn't hurt that Dave is a hunk—he's a basketball star, with a dazzling smile and a big heart.

April Winter has been to ten schools in the last ten years—and she hopes she's at Murphy to stay. Her energy, blond hair, and offbeat personality make her a standout at school.

And there's Billy Turner, José Melendez, and the rest of the gang. You'll meet them all in the halls of Murphy High and after school for a pizza at 18 Pine St.

One

"Well, it looks like my whole life has to be replanned," Kwame Brown said as he eased down into the booth at 18 Pine St. Cindy Phillips and Sarah Gordon sat across from him. Kwame was holding two slices of pizza, one in each hand, and a soft drink between his wrists.

"Kwame, it's bad enough that you sit down without being invited, but at least you could have asked us if we wanted anything." Cindy pushed her books aside so that Kwame would have room for his pizza. "And I didn't know you had already planned your entire life."

"Just the important things," Kwame said. "Tomorrow I'm going to have a test in English on *Death of a Salesman*. Whenever we have a test I come to 18 Pine, have two slices of pepperoni pizza, review for the test, and then get an A on it. With my A average I'll get a full scholarship to Howard, become a lawyer or a physicist, depending on what the job market looks like, marry Sarah, have three point five kids, and live happily ever after."

"Marry *who*?" Sarah leaned forward and rested her chin on her hand, looking at the short, stocky, mahogany-skinned boy with black-framed glasses. She liked Kwame as a friend, but marriage was definitely not on the agenda.

"I'm letting you in on my success express," Kwame said. "Anyway, when I reached the counter, Mr. Harris informed me that he did not have pepperoni pizza today. Instead there's a special on broccoli pizza. Which means I will probably not get an A on tomorrow's test, which means I will probably not get a full scholarship to Howard, which means I will have to spend an extra year in school and Sarah will have to work to support me while I get my law degree."

"Dream on, child." Sarah shook her head. "This woman is not going to work and support some man while he is in school. When you get your degree you can give me a call to see if I'm still available."

If you asked Sarah's best friend, Cindy Phillips, to describe Sarah, she'd probably start by telling you how caring and sensitive Sarah was. She'd talk about Sarah's warm smile, her dark skin, and her

2

sparkling eyes. The two of them spent so much time on the phone together that Sarah's mother was considering surgery to have it removed from Sarah's ear.

At seventeen, Sarah was the older of two sisters, and even though her little sister Allison was a pest sometimes, they got along all right. In fact, Sarah got along with almost everyone she met. She liked herself and she liked the people around her. Even though she was close to Kwame, Sarah wasn't really serious about boys. But lately, she'd felt feelings, especially about her friend Dave Hunter, that she'd never felt before.

"Sarah, check out José's sweater!" Cindy poked her best friend and looked in the direction of José Melendez, the handsome junior standing near the jukebox. He was wearing a light green sweater.

"Did I ever tell you that I would kill for that boy's eyelashes?" Sarah asked.

"On you, looking out, or on him, looking into your eyes?" Cindy asked.

"Girl, you do make me blush," Sarah responded.

"Must you people talk that girl talk when my whole life is in jeopardy?" Kwame asked.

"Kwame, you have already wolfed down one slice of pizza and you're halfway through the second, so you don't seem to be in that much distress," Sarah said. "Is it any good?"

"How can I tell after only two slices?" Kwame asked.

"We should enter Kwame in the talent contest as a world-class pizza eater," Cindy said.

"What talent contest?" Kwame said as he stuffed the last bite into his mouth.

"Yo, Sarah! Yo, Cindy! Yo, Kwame!" José pointed to each of them as he went past.

"Hey, José!" Sarah answered.

Kwame waved at José, and Cindy smiled shyly.

Cindy Phillips had lived in Madison since she had moved with her family from Jamaica at the age of three. Sarah had been her best friend for as long as she could remember. They'd been through a lot together, and it seemed as if their friendship just kept getting stronger.

Cindy had sparkling brown eyes, a "cute nose," according to Sarah, and beautiful dark brown skin. Of course she was crazy about boys. Even though she'd never had a serious boyfriend, she liked to think about having one.

"What talent contest?" Kwame repeated.

"My dad's trying to raise money to get video equipment for the kids at Hamilton. We're waiting to hear on his final request to the school board. If the money doesn't come through, the kids don't get the equipment," Sarah said. "I came up with the idea of holding a talent contest at Murphy. We'll charge admission and give the money to Dad for the equipment."

"What are they going to do with video stuff?" Cindy asked. "I thought the kids at Hamilton took mostly basic courses. You know, English and math, that kind of thing."

The town of Madison had two high schools, Murphy and Hamilton. Murphy was a mainstream school, with an emphasis on academics. Hamilton was for kids who needed extra attention—it offered remedial courses, a vocational program, and special programs for challenged students. In addition to teaching a math course, Sarah's father was the principal. Aside from a few kids who dropped by the Gordon home occasionally, Sarah didn't know any students from Hamilton.

"Dad said that's why the school board probably won't come up with the loot," Sarah said. "'Not part of the curriculum,' the board said."

"And that, ladies and gentlemen"—Kwame held a salt shaker up to his mouth as if it were a microphone—"is why Sarah Gordon, a junior from Madison's fabulous Murphy High, has stepped in to save the day."

"Kwame, do you have any hidden talent?" Cindy asked. "I mean I know you don't have any obvious talent. I just wondered."

"Hey, I'm crushed." Kwame stood up. "I walk into this place to have some pizza and instead I'm verbally harassed." Kwame knew he was smart when it came to books, but most of his confidence with girls was just an act. He was trying hard to be accepted as a person and a friend, not just the world's best homework helper.

5

"Well, what do you expect in a place that doesn't even have a name?" Sarah said. "But do sit down, you fine hunk of manliness."

"Fine hunk of manliness?" Kwame smiled. "At least the insults didn't cost me money. I've got a feeling that 'fine hunk of manliness' is definitely going to cost me something."

"Not money, just a little sweat. My dad's out of town, and he won't be back until Wednesday," Sarah said. "I want to finish as much as possible to surprise him when he gets back. I need somebody to make up some flyers. Can my fine hunk of manliness handle that awesome chore?"

"Well, since you put it that way, I will. But first, tell me two things," Kwame said, sitting down again. "What do you want on the flyer and how come your dad always splits when there's work to be done?"

"Please, Mr. Brown," Cindy said with the palms of her hands together. "Sarah's dad does not always split when there's work to be done. He had to go to Arizona to pick up Sarah's cousin."

"California." Sarah corrected Cindy. "Kwame, I'll let you know the where and when. But you fill in the rest. You know what a talent contest is. Use your imagination. I mean, sophomores do have imaginations, don't they?"

"Do you know what I imagine when I see you?" Kwame asked.

"No, I don't," Sarah said. "And if you tell me I'll

6

probably slap your face."

Kwame stood up and grinned broadly. "You probably would," he said.

"Kwame!" Sarah tossed a balled-up napkin at him.

"There goes a wasted youth," Cindy said as Kwame left.

"Yes, darling." Sarah wrapped a chunk of hair around her finger. "His immaturity is so...so...immature!" They both started laughing.

"And who is this creature coming across the floor?" Cindy asked.

"Do you mean she of the Best Label jeans and the blouse which she found in a cute little boutique for fifty zillion dollars?"

"One and the same," Cindy said, lowering her voice as Jennifer Wilson approached their table. Jennifer was tall and thin, with most of her hair pulled back in a bun—just enough was combed to the side to match the latest fashion she'd seen in one of the magazines. Clothes seemed tailor-made for Jennifer's trim figure and boyish hips, and Jennifer took full advantage.

"Hey, people." Jennifer sat down heavily. "I have just been put through an ordeal that you would not—I say again—you would not believe."

"What happened, Jennifer?" Sarah asked, even though she knew what was coming.

"I looked in over thirty stores for a pair of kick-arounds that would not put blisters on the Jennifer's feet."

7

"You find anything?" Sarah asked.

"Not in the mall," Jennifer said. "I left the mall and went over to Silver Lake and found this odd little shop—you wouldn't expect to find anything there—and finally found a pair of casuals that I could tolerate. Not actually like, mind you, but tolerate."

"How much were they?" Cindy asked, nudging Sarah under the table. Cindy and Sarah might be jealous of Jennifer's allowance, but they were both happy that their parents weren't divorced, like Jennifer's.

"A hundred and twelve," Jennifer said. "I would have paid twice that much just to end the search. And what's this I hear about Kwame working for your father?"

"Who told you that?" Sarah asked.

"He nearly knocked me over going out the door," Jennifer said. "I asked him where he was going and he said he was going to do some work for your father."

"What he's going to do is make up some flyers for the talent show," Cindy said. "Didn't Sarah tell you about it?"

"She did, and I'm trying to convince her that we need a category for shopping. It's *my* talent," Jennifer said with a laugh. "And speaking of shopping, don't you think this place is getting a bit noisy?"

"They're letting in too many freshmen," Cindy said. "I mentioned to Mr. Harris that he should be a

8

bit more selective about who he allows in here."

"When Dad gets back with my cousin I'll bring her here to introduce her to everybody," Sarah said. "I heard that if you put people into a new situation you should try to provide familiar surroundings. I assume they have pizza places in California."

"Run this cousin bit by me one more time." Jennifer had taken out her nail kit and was spreading the pieces across the table according to size. The cuticle pushers were on one end and the brushes were on the other.

"Jennifer, how come you don't just use the brushes that come in the polish?" Cindy asked.

"Mom gets this polish from a Japanese client," Jennifer said. "She did his whole house over in Art Deco and he gave her all these cosmetics."

"Which you promptly confiscated," Sarah said.

"Naturally," Jennifer replied.

"Is it expensive?" Cindy asked, nudging Sarah with her knee again.

"Don't ask!" Jennifer said, holding her nails to the light.

"I won't," Cindy said.

"Seven dollars a bottle," Jennifer said. "Now tell me about this cousin from California. Is this the one whose father played pro football?"

"Yeah, and now she's coming east to live with us," Sarah said.

"What's her name again?" Jennifer asked.

"Tasha," Sarah answered. Just saying her name

made Sarah a little nervous. Sarah hadn't seen Tasha in a long time. Sarah wondered what Tasha would be like, if she'd be troubled. Sarah didn't know anyone else whose parents had died—Tasha's mother and father had been killed a few years ago in a car accident.

"We'll just call her the Other Gordon," Cindy's voice interrupted her thoughts.

"Any way you look at it," Jennifer said, "having somebody move into your life like that has got to be a total trip. She's practically going to be your sister."

"Sort of," Sarah said. She remembered the first conversation she had had with her father about the situation. Her father had said that she would probably love having someone her own age to talk with and "pal around" with. But Sarah wasn't sure. Her junior year at Murphy High was turning out to be difficult enough with all the questions about what she was going to do with the rest of her life. And now a new person to deal with, to think about, to share her life with, when she wasn't at all sure anymore what that life was about. And Tasha had to have questions and problems of her own. It was not something Sarah enjoyed thinking about.

"Sarah, are you awake?" Cindy interrupted Sarah's thoughts. "What are you thinking about?"

"Sorry." Sarah tried to bring her attention back to her friends. "I guess I haven't given this a lot of thought, but having Tasha live with us is really going to change my life."

10

"How old is this girl?" Jennifer asked.

"Seventeen, same age as us." Sarah said.

"How well do you know her?" Cindy asked.

"I met her once when we were five. My dad and my uncle never got along that well," Sarah said.

"Five was a long time ago," Jennifer said, "which means you don't know her. She didn't like boys, the most important thing in life."

"*Au contraire*, my friend," Cindy said. "Tomorrow we are having a test on *A Separate Peace*, and that is the important stuff of life for the next sixteen hours."

"Cindy." Jennifer put down her nail file carefully. "I realize that your parents are from Jamaica and you do not understand the ways of the mainland. But here in the U.S. of A., we do not mention tests on books that our friends have not yet read."

"You haven't even read it yet?" Sarah asked. "How did you get the paper done?"

"Girlfriend, I wanted to talk to you about that very thing," Jennifer said. "I'll walk you home."

Bright autumn leaves whipped around Sarah's ankles as she walked down Pine toward the Madison Public Library. She didn't have a reason to go to the library but she didn't want to go home, either. There were things that needed thinking about—things like colleges, and grades, and friends, and parents, and boys. She hadn't thought too much about boys in the past year, but for a lot of the girls that seemed to be

11

the only thing on their minds. She hadn't thought too much about her parents, either. They had always been there for her, sometimes in ways that she wasn't aware of, like paying the bills, but now they were always asking her questions about what schools she was going to apply to, what she wanted to do with her life.

She didn't know the answer to most of the questions they were asking. And for some reason she wanted to have some answers before her unknown cousin, Tasha, became a live-in member of her family.

Two

"Mrs. Gordon, we have a legal problem and we need your advice." Cindy had arrived at the Gordon household at seven. "We picked out a pair of jeans for me last weekend at the mall."

"In good faith," Sarah said, plopping a spoonful of smooth peanut butter in the center of an English muffin.

"Sarah, I will pay you not to put jam and peanut butter on an English muffin." Mrs. Gordon peered over her coffee cup at her older daughter. Sarah had her mother's eyes and skin, but everyone said she got her smile from her father.

"I'm just balancing the carbohydrates," Sarah said. "Let Cindy tell you what happened with the jeans."

13

"Go ahead, Cindy."

"When I bought these jeans, they fit just perfectly, for off the rack. See?" Cindy turned gracefully in a small circle, modeling the jeans for Mrs. Gordon. "We bought this fuschia shirt, too."

"Well, I see that it's a nice combination," Mrs. Gordon said. "And the pants look like a pretty good fit to me."

"They're supposed to shrink, Mom," Sarah explained patiently. "Cindy washed them nine times and they still haven't shrunk."

"Oh, I see," Mrs. Gordon nodded. "You want them to shrink so that they hug in all the right places. So that you have to fight your way into them. So that all the boys go crazy when you go by and you can become '*really disgusted*' with them for being so crude."

"You got it, Mrs. G.!" Cindy said, laughing. Her laugh was so good-natured that Mrs. Gordon joined her.

"Well, does she have a case or not?" Sarah asked, spreading strawberry jam on her muffin.

"I seriously doubt it. Most clothing manufacturers supply a guarantee against shrinkage, not for it." Mrs. Gordon got up from the table and walked to the sink. "Case closed. Now get a move on. You're going to be late for school."

"I'm ready, just making sure I am nutritionally prepared." Sarah began to load another muffin with jam and peanut butter. At the sound of the phone

14

ringing, she dropped the muffin and raced toward the phone.

Cindy beat her to it. "Gordon residence," she announced in her best British accent.

Sarah returned to the table and picked up her muffin. She watched Cindy listening to the caller. "Just a moment, Jennifer," Cindy said and then covered the mouthpiece. "Sarah, Jennifer wants to know if you have a copy of your paper for English that she can borrow."

Before Sarah could answer, Mrs. Gordon gave her daughter a sharp look.

"Um, tell her that I'll have to think about it," Sarah said slowly.

Mrs. Gordon frowned.

Cindy quickly relayed Sarah's message and replaced the phone on the hook.

"She just wants to take a look at it, Mom," Sarah said. "Did Dad call last night? What time is he coming home?"

"Don't try to change the subject, young lady," Mrs. Gordon said firmly as Allison Gordon bounced into the room. The bill of Allison's orange baseball cap rested lightly against the collar of her denim shirt.

"Allison's only eleven and I don't think she would lend her papers to her classmates. Right, dear?" Mrs. Gordon took the baseball cap from her daughter's head as she passed and hooked it on the back of the nearest chair.

"Of course Mom is right," Allison said, her eyes scanning the table for signs of breakfast food. "But without naming names, it is also true that I've always had a higher moral standard than some people."

"Stuff it, pipsqueak." Sarah drained the juice from her glass and checked her chartreuse mini-jumper for crumbs. "Mom, can you drop Cindy and me off at school on your way to work?"

"If you get a move on," Mrs. Gordon answered.

"How come Sarah gets a ride when she asks and you always tell me no?" Allison asked.

"That's because you are an unloved child." Sarah snatched Allison's orange juice and drank it before her sister could react. "And a slow child." Sarah really loved her little sister, even if she felt she was an overachieving pest.

"Mom, you and Dad really messed up on your first try. Sarah has strong criminal tendencies." Allison got up from the table and headed for the dishwasher. "I'm glad you got it right the second time," she added with a giggle.

"When is Mr. G. coming home?" Cindy took a comb from her handbag and began to fluff her hair.

"This afternoon, and he's bringing Tasha with him," Mrs. Gordon said.

"We've got the guest room fixed up for her," Allison said, rescuing her cap from the back of the chair. "It looks great."

"Allison go and tell your grandmother that we're leaving."

"Okay, but I just remembered I promised Pamela that I would walk to school with her this morning. She's going out for soccer this year and wants to start training early." Allison pecked her mother on the cheek and left the kitchen.

"Be home early," Mrs. Gordon said. She took her keys from the pegboard on the wall. "Let's get started, girls." In addition to being a successful attorney, Mrs. Gordon was also a successful mother, at least according to her two kids. Despite her heavy workload, she always managed to be around for the important things.

Mrs. Gordon walked to the car, opened the door of the boxy sedan, and slid in. She smiled as she adjusted the mirror and watched Sarah and Cindy climb into the backseat. The two girls had been friends since kindergarten. If the saying that opposites attract ever needed verifying, Mrs. Gordon thought that these two were a perfect example. Sarah was tall and slender, her skin the color of dark chocolate. Her smile was electric.

If Mrs. Gordon were to use one word to describe Cindy's appearance, it would be "spicy." Cindy was petite, several inches shorter than Sarah, and well shaped. Her hair was dark brown and she wore it in thin braids, sometimes bunching it into a multilayered ponytail. Her skin had a glow that made her seem radiant.

But if they were opposites in appearance, they were like twins when it came to their personalities. Mrs. Gordon wished she had a nickel for every hour the two had spent on the phone together, discussing everything and nothing, all in great detail.

"That hat you're wearing is nice," Cindy said as the car turned out into the street.

"I made it from that kente cloth Dad bought me last year," Sarah said.

"Your dad said that Tasha has grown into quite a young woman," Mrs. Gordon said.

"I'm going to let her help me with the talent show," Sarah said. "The work will be good for her."

"Could be," Mrs. Gordon said. "I was telling your father you're following through with your plan and he was pleased. Sounds like a lot of work, though." Mrs. Gordon's voice trailed off as they neared the school. "Quite a crowd outside. Do any of you ever go *inside*?"

"Very funny, Mom! We're early and the girls are checking each other out, seeing what everybody is wearing," Sarah said.

"And the boys are checking out the girls," Cindy added.

"And then you check out the boys who were checking you out, right?" Mrs. Gordon said, pulling the car to the curb.

"You got it, Moms."

Kwame leaned down and looked in the open car window. "*Bonjour*, Madame Gordon and entourage."

"*Bonjour* yourself, Kwame Brown." Mrs. Gordon reached through the window and shook his hand. "How are your parents? Are they still playing bridge?"

"They're fine and they've just entered a duplicate tournament." Kwame stepped back and opened the rear door for the girls. He bowed grandly as they exited.

"Sarah, I'd like you to come straight home after school," Mrs. Gordon said. "It would be nice if you were there to greet your cousin when she and your father arrive."

"I'll be there, Mom," Sarah said.

As they started toward the side door of Murphy High, Sarah wondered again what Tasha would be like. Sarah had always watched Tasha's father play football on television, rarely missing a game. Then, when she heard about the accident, she stopped watching football altogether.

It had been so long since Sarah had seen Tasha. There was no telling what she'd be like. But she was blood, and it was good that their worlds were coming together. Really good, Sarah told herself with not too many doubts.

Three

"The one thing half decent in the cafeteria are these raisin buns," Kwame said as he leaned his head back and dropped a frosted piece into his mouth.

"Speaking of buns, take a quick peek at the new guy sitting near the window. He's gorgeous." Jennifer Wilson rolled her eyes in delight.

"He doesn't look that good to me," Kwame said. "And besides, he couldn't possibly come between us, could he?"

"Us? Us? There is no us. There is me and the rest of civilization and then there is you," Jennifer said teasingly.

"Why must I endure such pain?" Kwame moaned.

"Hi, everyone. Move over, Kwame." Cindy carried a tray in each hand. She put them on the table and sat next to Kwame.

"You're eating two lunches?" Kwame asked. "And I wouldn't touch those raisin buns if I were you." He smiled at Cindy.

"This is April's tray. She's over in the snack line getting yogurt," Cindy said. "The girl eats like a horse and doesn't put on a pound."

"How old is she?" Sarah asked.

"She's sixteen going on twenty," Cindy said.

"We should make her our salvation project for this year," Sarah said.

"Make me your salvation project and fix me up with the new guy," Jennifer countered.

"Hey, everyone." April Winter smiled radiantly at the group as she squeezed in between Sarah and Jennifer.

"April, you look like you should be somewhere leading a cheer," Cindy said. "Didn't anybody tell you that perky is out this year?"

"Don't worry, as soon as I get my braces off I'm adopting a new image," April said. "I'm going to be a Woman of the Shadows. Maybe I'll learn to sing the blues."

"I've never heard of a sixteen-year-old white blues singer," Kwame said.

"I'll be the first," April said, making a face at him.

"Then you're definitely going to have to get rid of those pink glasses," Jennifer said. "And you're going to have to do something about your hair, too."

21

April forced herself to smile. She had promised herself she would not be so gung ho this year, that she would calm down. But every time she thought about the fact that she was a sophomore and friends with the coolest group of juniors in the school, she just started talking like a parrot on caffeine. "Yeah, I know," she said. "Maybe I'll get a wig."

"Your hair is fine," Sarah said. "I like it. We're all just teasing you."

"Thanks." April started a grin, remembered her braces, and settled for a smile that hid her teeth. She decided that the bangs would get chopped on her next trip for a haircut.

"We're checking out the new guy near the window," Sarah said.

April twisted around in her seat to see who they were talking about. "Oh, that's Roy Edwards," she said. "He managed a rock group in Detroit and he's living with his uncle here in Madison to learn how to produce records."

"Say *what*?" Cindy asked.

Everyone at the table looked at April in surprise and with a bit of admiration.

"How do you know that?" Jennifer asked suspiciously.

"He gave me a lift to school this morning," April said smiling.

"No!" Cindy lifted an eyebrow.

"Yeah, he lives in the same condo complex I do," April said. "He saw my Murphy High jacket and asked me if I needed a lift."

"So, April, when do you want me to go home with you and replan your wardrobe?" Jennifer asked sweetly.

"She can't do that until I finish helping her with her math," Sarah said.

"Ladies, get back. You know I'm spending the week with April." Cindy added, joining in the fun.

"You girls are nuts," Kwame said, putting his books back into his pack. "At least I can talk to my homeboy."

"Hello, hello, hello." Dave Hunter sauntered over to the table and put out both hands, palms up, for Kwame to slap. Dave Hunter was tall and powerfully built. He kept his tightly curled hair cut short, and his dark skin made his intense eyes seem even more intense. Dave didn't consider himself all that attractive, but many of the girls at Murphy disagreed.

"What's up, Dave?" Cindy asked.

"Nothing much," Dave said. "We're supposed to have our first basketball practice this afternoon and I'm kind of anxious to see how the freshmen play."

As Dave talked about the basketball team, Sarah began to think about what had happened the week before. She and Dave had been friends since their mothers took them to the sandbox together when they were just learning to walk.

They lived across the street from each other and had shared neighborhood barbecues, swim parties, church picnics, and school functions for as long as they could remember. But one day this past summer, after having a water fight while washing Mrs. Gordon's car, everything had suddenly changed. It had shaken them both.

Sarah had been drying Dave's back and telling him about a dumb trick that Allison had tried on her. He had laughed, and suddenly the strong chin had seemed stronger and his even, white teeth had seemed whiter. At first she had tried to ignore the feelings that stirred and unsettled her. She had rubbed his shoulder harder, and then, without her thinking about it, she had kissed the shoulder lightly. He had turned and looked into her eyes and she had looked away quickly.

"I'm s-sorry," she had stammered.

"Sorry?" He had touched her hand and she had pulled it away.

They had exchanged embarrassed smiles, and Sarah had made some excuse to go into her house. They had smiled and waved to each other, but both of them had known that they would never look at each other in the same way again.

The sound of the period bell sent students scattering and scurrying to get to the next class. Snatches of conversation filled the hall.

"Meet me at my locker."

"Who have you got for sixth period?"

"I've got PE last period."

Students moved in random bursts of energy and

motion through the large double doors that separated the old part of the school from the new wing. Different textures of hair and a rainbow of skin colors and clothing blossomed in the halls of Murphy High.

The afternoon went by too fast for Sarah. She didn't want to admit it, but she was getting nervous about seeing Tasha.

"Don't think that we have formal meals like this every day." Sarah and Allison's grandmother placed the bowl of steamed red potatoes in front of Tasha. "Matter of fact," she continued, "this is the first time I've seen this family all in one place in a long time."

"Remember last Saturday we all watched the news together on television, Miss Essie," Allison said. "We thought a friend of Sarah's was going to be on," she told Tasha.

"The mother of one of Sarah's friends won a big contract to decorate an embassy in Washington," Mrs. Gordon said.

"They went to her house and interviewed her and everything but it didn't make the news," Allison cut in before Sarah could say a word.

"The forest fire might have been a bit more important than Mrs. Wilson's decorating plans." Mr. Gordon's measured baritone voice reflected the years he'd spent singing in church and with the university choir. His face shone with pride as he looked around the table at his family. In addition to being the principal at Hamilton, he looked like a principal.

Mr. Gordon was tall, with a serious face and a kind smile. His skin was lighter than Sarah's—she could see where Tasha's complexion came from. His horn rim glasses completed the package.

"I still can't get over how much Tasha looks like you, Donald," Mrs. Gordon said.

"I was shocked myself." Tasha Gordon's husky voice seemed too heavy for her thin frame. "I opened the door and almost fainted. It was a shocker all right."

Sarah could not help staring at her cousin; she was that beautiful. Words like "stunning," "sophisticated," and "sexy" all fit her nicely. The leopard print jumpsuit she wore seemed made for her figure, and her long hair framed her face dramatically. Sarah couldn't imagine letting her hair grow that long, nor could she imagine having three holes pierced in each earlobe. The tiny jeweled studs in Tasha's ears twinkled in the Gordon dining room. Sarah had heard the word "exotic" used to describe people before, but she'd never known what it meant.

"Madison might not be as exciting as Oakland," Mr. Gordon was saying, "but I think it's a city that's making a lot of progress, and Murphy High has a good reputation."

"What's the story with this other school, the one that you're the principal of, Uncle Donald?"

"Well, Murphy High is a school for the bright, deserving kids in this city that don't need that much help making it from day to day." Mr. Gordon spoke slowly about his favorite subject. "But a lot of students who I think are equally bright and equally deserving were falling through the cracks at Murphy. Hamilton is the place for those kids. Some are academically in trouble, some are learning-disabled, and some just need a little more caring for."

"We're going to hold a talent contest at Murphy to raise money for them," Sarah said. "You can help. My friends are dying to meet you. I mean, I've told them all about you."

"*What*? What have you told them?" Tasha's husky voice sounded icy. "You hardly know me yourself." Her reaction startled Sarah.

"I just told them..." Sarah felt uncertain. "About your...you know...your situation."

"My situation? Sarah, I appreciate your wanting to be friendly but believe me, I don't intend to be anyone's pet project. And I don't travel in groups."

"I don't think Sarah meant any harm," Mrs. Gordon said. "She knows it's hard moving from one environment to another and I think she is trying to make your adjustment easier. You two are getting off on the wrong foot—I'm going to give you some time to work it out on your own."

"I'm sorry, Aunt Liz. I was under the impression that you guys had lived here all your life. Sarah doesn't know about moving from one environment to another." Tasha put her fork down beside her plate.

"I meant that Sarah, and the *entire* family, are

concerned for your well-being." Sarah couldn't remember her mother sounding so uncomfortable.

"I appreciate all of you being concerned and I thank you. Uncle Donald and Miss Essie are all that I have left of my father's family and I wanted to get to know them. However, I think this would be easier on us all, if all of you were a little less concerned. My parents left me well taken care of and I made it very clear to Uncle Donald that I expected to pay my own way here. Please don't think of me as a charity case."

"Tasha, please," Mr. Gordon said softly. "It's a new situation for all of us. We all have to work to make the transition."

"Of course." Tasha stood up. "It's been a long day for me. Do you mind if I turn in for the night?"

"No, of course not," Mrs. Gordon said.

"Daddy, I—I didn't mean to offend her." Sarah felt as if she was going to cry. She looked to her mother and father for support.

"That's okay, baby. It's just that things are still a bit raw with her and we're going to have to take it slow." Mr. Gordon reached over and squeezed Sarah's arm.

"She's proud and so unsure of herself," Miss Essie said. "Let's give her time."

"I like Tasha. I think she's cool," Allison said.

"That she is," Mrs. Gordon said. "Tasha's been through a lot. We need to work hard to make her feel like part of the family. Let's finish our dinner or

Miss Essie will get angry at us. She hates it when we don't eat dessert."

Miss Essie had once been a Broadway actress, and had appeared on television once or twice. Her career wasn't much any more, and Miss Essie spent most of her time sitting in the house or going for walks. She was a large woman, with gray hair and a smile that twinkled. Miss Essie walked slowly, but always stood straight and with dignity.

"I remember one time I invited my theater group to dinner," Miss Essie said with a broad smile. "They tried to leave before I served my famous pecan pie. I had to break a few legs before I convinced them to stay."

"Do you expect us to believe that Miss Essie?" Sarah asked.

"No, but if you do I've got a few more stories for you!"

"Mom, you are something else," Mr. Gordon said.

"We all are," Miss Essie said. "You just have to take a little time to figure us out."

Sarah knew that Miss Essie was talking about giving Tasha a little more time to warm up to her new situation. She would try to give Tasha all the time and the space she needed.

Four

"Sarah, get the door, honey." Miss Essie was braiding Allison's hair, a Saturday-morning ritual, when the doorbell rang.

Sarah took the magazine she was reading with her, trying to finish the article before she got to the door.

"Sarah, open the door!" Her mother said, laughing.

The short man standing on the Gordon porch said hello and smiled broadly. "Mr. Parrish to see Mr. Gordon," he announced. "I'm with the school board."

"Oh, come in." As Sarah stood aside to let Mr. Parrish in she saw her father appear from the den

30

and gesture toward their visitor.

"Carl," Mr. Gordon said as he shook hands. "What brings you here on a Saturday morning?"

"I was working on the budget estimates for next year," Mr. Parrish said, smiling. "I just wondered if you had completed your estimates."

"Come in, and have a seat," Donald Gordon said. "You've met my mother, I believe."

"Charmed," Mr. Parrish said, bowing slightly from the waist toward Miss Essie.

Sarah had the distinct impression that he was not at all charmed by either Miss Essie or anyone else.

"The estimates I submitted to the school board last week were final as far as I'm concerned," Mr. Gordon said.

"I understand that you submitted a separate request for video equipment," Mr. Parrish said. "I was talking to the mayor yesterday—you know he's really worried about the budget gap—and we even discussed the possibility of cutting the budget for the elementary school's library and the media center for Murphy High."

"The video equipment I asked for is something I think will benefit the students," Mr. Gordon said. "That does seem to be our job as educators, doesn't it, to help the students?"

"Of course," Mr. Parrish said. "I just wondered what priorities we should use. You know, when the mayor is saying that he can't even maintain the city's buses, it's going to be hard to ask him for extra money for television cameras for the Hamilton kids to play with."

Mr. Gordon's jaw tightened and relaxed several times.

"Well, there's a possibility that we can help raise the money for the video equipment," Mr. Gordon said. "We're still working on it."

"I don't think your supplemental request for board money is going to work," Mr. Parrish said. "If you think it's important, you'll have to raise that money yourself."

"I think anything that helps education is important," Mr. Gordon said. "It's up to the school board and the community to decide where we'll put our priorities."

"Yes, yes, of course. I think you understand where our priorities are." Mr. Parrish was smiling as he stood. "Well, I'll have to be on my way. You have a lovely home and a lovely family."

"Thank you." Mr. Gordon stood.

"Good day, ladies." Mr. Parrish bowed again, and in a moment was gone.

"What was that all about?" Miss Essie asked.

"He wanted to know about the school budget," Allison volunteered.

"Looked to me like he wanted more than that," Miss Essie said, separating the pieces of Allison's hair with her fingers. "Reminded me of one of those Florida alligators—showing his teeth and making believe it's a smile."

32

"I think he was nice," Allison said.

"You think *everyone*'s nice," Sarah said.

"Your grandmother's right," Donald Gordon said. "He's been against the very concept of Hamilton High since it began."

"Why, Daddy?" Sarah had picked up her magazine and now put it down again.

"He's the kind of person who feels he has to show that he's mainstream America by putting down people he thinks don't measure up," Mr. Gordon said. "If you give him half a chance he'll give you the whole story about how he 'pulled himself up by his bootstraps' and never needed a helping hand."

"Seems to me there are a lot of people in the world like that, people who forget that the world's not filled with people as perfect as they think they are," Miss Essie said. "Hold still, Allison!"

"I'm holding still, Miss Essie," Allison said, wincing. "But you're pulling my braids too tight."

"And what did he say about buses?" Sarah asked.

"There was a bit of a stink down at city hall last week about the maintenance of the buses owned by the city," Mr. Gordon said. "But if it wasn't about the buses it would be something else. That's the way the man is."

"We can raise the money for the video equipment without him. I already talked to the kids at school about it," Sarah said.

The front door opened and Tasha came in with a pile of books under her arm. "Hi, folks!" She

33

dropped the books in a chair and bent over to look at Allison's braids. "Looking good."

"Doing research?" Sarah asked.

"Started it," Tasha answered. "Hope to finish it sometime this weekend."

"What are you researching?" Allison asked.

"The causes of World War One," Tasha said. "Anyone notice if the refrigerator was still working?"

"It's working," Miss Essie said. "And there's macaroni and cheese from last night."

"So what caused the war?" Allison asked as Tasha headed for the kitchen.

Sarah listened for a while as her cousin began to explain the causes of World War I. Then she went to her room and started calling around. Since the board had refused the funding, they needed to start right away. It was 10:38 when she made the first call to Kwame, to make sure he was working on the flyer, and by noon she had promises from José to play flute, from Jennifer to model, and from three other juniors to either sing or dance. The seniors she called were a bit more reluctant, but she figured she would get them involved if she spoke to them personally at Murphy.

On Monday she succeeded in getting several of the seniors to promise they would help. She felt confident as she started home, saw some of her friends sitting at the edge of the athletic field, and headed toward them.

"Hi, guys!" Sarah spoke to Kwame and Dave. They were sitting on the grass watching the girls' soccer team practice. Sarah plopped down between the two boys, and Kwame moved over to give her space as Dave concentrated on the game.

"She's great," Kwame said, motioning toward the swirl of bodies on the field.

"Who, may I ask, is the object of your scrutiny?" Sarah poked Kwame playfully in the ribs.

"You don't know?" Dave laughed. "It's your cousin Tasha. Poor Kwame has fallen hard."

"What! You Kwame? Fallen hard? I don't believe this." To Sarah, it seemed as if Kwame had always had a crush on her. Neither one took it too seriously, though. Now it looked as if Kwame had decided that if he couldn't have Sarah, he'd try for her cousin.

Sarah shielded her eyes and peered toward the field. Tasha was playing center halfback. From where she sat Sarah could see the intensity on her cousin's face. The ball was put into play, and there was a brief blur of bodies from which Tasha emerged, pushing the ball ahead of her down the sidelines. A defender moved toward her and Tasha headed for the taller girl. She faked going left, slowed down for a moment, and kicked a hard shot that seemed to go almost through the defender, curve toward the net, and enter it just beyond the frantic dive of the goalie. A cheer went up among Tasha's teammates.

"She's good," Kwame said, his voice full of admi-

35

ration. Sarah couldn't believe it. Kwame was everybody's buddy, but he had never expressed a personal interest in any girl except Sarah, and that always seemed like a joke.

Kwame was always talking about some scientific discovery, or politics, or book collecting. He had started collecting books written about the role of African-Americans in the Civil War. He also collected Civil War memorabilia. At first they had kidded him about his war posters and other odd artifacts, but as his collection grew so did everyone's respect for him.

Sarah glanced over at Dave, but he was watching the field. "Yes, she is good," Sarah mumbled.

"Well, how does it feel to have such a gorgeous cousin?" Dave said and looked over at her.

"You think Tasha is gorgeous?" Sarah picked at the tufts of grass. She refused to meet Dave's eye.

"Yeah, don't you?" Dave watched as the ball moved away from them down the field.

Tasha scored another goal and Dave and Kwame gave each other high fives. The coach blew the whistle and the practice broke up. Sarah watched Tasha joke around with her teammates. It had been less than a week since Tasha had arrived and she acted as if she had been at Murphy all her life. Sarah wondered how she could ever have been worried about Tasha adjusting to a new situation. She was about to get up when she realized that Tasha was headed their way.

"That was a workout and a half." Tasha wiped the sweat from her forehead with a bright kerchief that was around her neck. She sat down on the grass next to Kwame.

"You looked good out there," Kwame said.

"Thanks, K.B." Tasha smiled at him.

Kwame looked flustered. Sarah was surprised. Nothing, but nothing, ever blew Kwame's cool.

"I didn't know you were on the soccer team," Sarah said.

"I'm not, officially," Tasha said, stretching out on the grass. "This is sort of a tryout for me. I've already missed a couple of practices, but the coach said it was okay. The high school I went to in California won the state championship."

"So, you're like a girl jock?" Dave asked with interest.

"Yeah," Tasha said, shading her eyes as she looked up at him. "Does that mean we've got something in common?" she asked teasingly.

Sarah started to fume. She had told Tasha all about Dave, all about their friendship and the way it was developing into something more. And now it looked as if her cousin was flirting with him. She didn't know what to say.

"You play basketball, Tasha?" Kwame asked, but before she could answer, Dave jumped in.

"Our girls' basketball team could use some help."

Sarah was quick to defend the team. "They're not so bad. They won a few games last year."

37

"Yeah, two to be exact," Kwame said.

"Ouch!" Tasha said, propping herself up on one elbow. "They do need help. I may look into it."

Before Sarah could reply she heard Cindy's, Jennifer's, and April's voices. She looked behind her. The three of them were coming toward them, waving and yelling. Sarah was relieved to have her girlfriends with her.

"Hey, you guys having a meeting?" April called out.

"Just don't vote until we sit down," Cindy joined in.

"Somebody is going to have to loan me their jacket to sit on," Jennifer said. "I simply can't get grass stains on my skirt."

Tasha pulled her sweatjacket from her pile and tossed it to Jennifer. It seemed to Sarah that the boys must have been guarding Tasha's books and clothes while she practiced. Sarah felt a tightness in her chest. If Tasha seriously liked Dave, she didn't know what she'd do.

"Thanks," Jennifer said, sitting. "Tasha, you are in great shape," she observed.

"Yeah, she is," Kwame said appreciatively and everyone laughed. Sarah noticed that no one seemed surprised to see Kwame fawning all over Tasha.

Cindy sat down and began retying her scarf.

"Three weeks into the semester and Mrs. Bender is starting to mess with me," Jennifer complained.

"Then do your work," Tasha offered pleasantly.

"Excuse me?" Jennifer looked surprised. Her

38

mother and grandmother both had gone to prestigious black women's colleges in the South. There was no doubt in Jennifer's mind that she would follow, and with a minimum of work.

"Do the work," Tasha repeated.

"I am doing my work, Ms. Gordon," Jennifer said evenly.

"Then do it right and do it yourself and do it on time." Tasha's tone held no sarcasm, just firm advice.

"Just who shined your halo this morning?" Jennifer's voice was sharp.

"Nobody shined my halo," Tasha said, sitting up and crossing her legs. "But I don't see why you're complaining when you know you're half-stepping."

Jennifer was speechless. No one her age had ever spoken to her like that. She looked around the group for support. "Well, I guess I could do a little more," she said, the corners of her mouth tightening.

Tasha started pushing her things into her backpack. "Hey, guys, Miss Essie is going to her drama club meeting tonight, and Aunt Liz and Uncle Donald are both going to be late. Sooo," she said, smiling, "I'm cooking. How about all of you coming over and eating a vegetarian lasagna dish?"

"No meat?" April asked suspiciously, looking around at the others.

"No meat and fantastic!" Tasha kissed the tips of her fingers. They all laughed. "Come on gang, be brave," she urged.

"What time?" Dave asked.

"Six all right?" Tasha asked. "What do you think, Sarah?"

"Okay with me, I guess," Sarah said.

"Then six it is." Tasha stood and threw her bag over her shoulder.

"You got it." Kwame scrambled to his feet. "I'll see you guys tonight."

"Is this our Kwame?" Sarah asked as she watched Kwame almost hopping along next to Tasha.

"'Fraid so," Jennifer said, smiling. "I think it's cute."

"Me, too," Cindy said, gathering up her books.

"How long has this been going on?" Sarah tried to keep the indignation out of her voice. These were her friends and suddenly she was the last to know everything.

"Since the first day you introduced them," Dave said. "Your cousin's one smooth lady. Well, if I'm coming to your house tonight for vegetarian what-have-you, I'd better get home and into the shower."

"Yes indeedy," Jennifer said, tossing Tasha's sweatjacket to Sarah. "We'd better all get our acts together for the Other Gordon."

Sarah was thinking salad. If Tasha was going to make vegetarian lasagna, then she would make the best salad the gang had ever had. She was thinking salad when she got home and heard Tasha singing in the shower, and she was thinking salad as she checked the refrigerator for lettuce. She was still thinking salad when the phone rang.

"Hello?"

"Sarah?"

"Yeah, Kwame." Sarah put two heads of lettuce on the counter as she talked.

"I'm going to be a little late," Kwame said.

"Good, we'll eat everything before you get here," Sarah teased.

"Hey, Sarah?"

"Hey, Kwame?"

"You know, I didn't get those flyers copied." Kwame's voice sounded suddenly distant.

"No big thing," Sarah said. "But we need them out soon. Can you get it done tomorrow?"

"Uh—Tasha doesn't think it's a good idea for us to have a talent show," Kwame said. "She said maybe we should talk about it tonight."

"She said *what*?"

"That maybe there was a better way of dealing with the problem and that we could discuss it at dinner," Kwame said. "Look, I have to run an errand for my mom. I'll see you later."

When Sarah hung up she was furious. She had planned the talent contest and had got things started to raise the money for the video equipment. She had figured if enough kids participated in the contest most of the school would turn out for it. At a price of just a few dollars for admission they could get a good start on the equipment for the kids at Hamilton.

Just who did Tasha think she was?

Sarah put the lettuce back into the refrigerator and went into her room. She slipped a compact disc of Bob Marley into the CD player, put on the headphones, and turned up the volume. She needed to do some serious drowning out of some of the things she was thinking. She made a decision, just after the very disturbing thought of strangling Tasha with her bare hands, that she wouldn't say anything until dinner; then she would defend her idea. After all, it was her father's school that needed the equipment, and Tasha was living in her father's house.

Five

Sarah hadn't made a salad but Tasha had. Sarah looked around the dinner table at her friends and at Roy Edwards. She didn't know how Tasha had managed to meet the new guy but there he was, charcoal-gray slacks, black shirt, and a voice that seemed just too smooth to be coming from a guy from Madison. Sarah remembered that Roy was from Detroit, and had managed a rock group. Maybe, she thought, the smoothness went along with the territory. Everyone seemed to be having a great time. She put a forkful of Tasha's cucumber and onion salad in her mouth and pretended not to like it.

"This sauce is terrific." Allison licked her lips and used her bread to soak up the excess on her plate. "I never knew spaghetti sauce could taste this good." Eleven-year-old Allison didn't get to hang out with Sarah's friends too often, and she was enjoying every moment.

"Tell me about it." Jennifer touched the corners of her mouth daintily with her napkin. "And I could certainly stand another slice of garlic bread."

"But can your hips?" Cindy asked, reaching for the last slice.

April giggled at Cindy's quip and crunched on a crisp radish. Dave and Kwame lifted big pieces of cheese-covered lasagna on their forks.

"I love a woman who knows her way around a kitchen," Roy announced pleasantly. "I mean, some women seem to get embarrassed if they know how to make tea."

When Roy had first arrived, he had stood around looking uncomfortable for a brief moment until Tasha had given him the task of slicing onions for the salad. Roy's smooth, dark-chocolate skin was stretched tautly over his bony face, which reminded Sarah of an African sculpture she had once seen in a museum. His eyes, which looked sullen and fierce, were never still.

"So what's it like managing a rock group?" Jennifer asked.

"More work than you'd think," Roy responded. "At least it was more work than I'd bargained for. Half the time I was either carrying bags or loading and unloading amplifiers. Until a group gets famous,

44

the manager does all the work."

"Did the group you manage dance?" Cindy asked.

"They had a few little steps," Roy answered. "Nothing fantastic."

Sarah wondered if he had said that because he was a dancer. She had already noticed how gracefully he moved. "Allison, you'd better get upstairs and finish your homework," Sarah said, looking pointedly at the clock on the mantel. "Mom and Dad will be home soon."

"In a while," Allison protested. She was hanging on every word being said around the table. This dinner—without grown-ups—seemed like a special event, and she wanted to be a part of it.

"Allison, why don't you finish your homework and then come down and have dessert with us? I've got a special treat," Tasha said.

"She's not supposed to have sweets late at night." Sarah resented Tasha's butting in.

"No sweets," Tasha said. "It's fresh fruit with yogurt chips."

Allison started upstairs with a promise to be back as soon as she had finished her assignments.

"I thought now would be a great time to talk about the talent show," Tasha said. "You seem to have a lot of ideas, Sarah."

"So do you, apparently," Sarah responded. "I don't see a reason for discussing it. I thought my plans were already final."

"Well, I can see your point about the talent contest, Sarah, and I think it's an interesting idea," Tasha said.

"Yes, it would give the kids at Murphy an opportunity to show off their talents," Cindy said.

"That's the thing that bothers me," Tasha said. "Why should we hold a fund-raiser, or a talent contest, for the kids at Hamilton? I mean, they're the ones who want the video equipment. Or at least that's what Kwame was saying. Is that right, Kwame?"

"I think so," Kwame said, his head down.

"So why are *we* putting on the show?" Tasha repeated.

"Because we care about them," Sarah said. "And I'm sure that we can do a good job of it."

"That's very noble," Tasha said dryly.

"So what do you want to do?" April asked.

"It's their school. Let them handle it," Tasha said. "If we want to do something for Murphy we should do something for Murphy."

"So you're against doing this for Hamilton?" Cindy asked.

"To get it right up front, I am," Tasha said. "I think that maybe we can offer them some ideas, but I don't think we should do it for them. They're not a charity, you know."

"They could picket the school board," April said.

"Or put on their own talent show," Tasha said.

"Hey, Sarah, get a notebook and start writing some of this stuff down," Kwame said. "We don't want to miss anything."

46

Sarah got up and went to the desk in the hall. She felt defeated. It seemed that somewhere along the line her brainchild had been kidnapped and given a facelift.

"You all right?" Cindy had seen Sarah's face when she left the room and had followed her to the hall. She put her hand on Sarah's shoulder.

"Yeah, I'm fine." Sarah widened her eyes to keep the tears from forming. "Cindy, she just makes me feel so jealous and I don't like feeling like this. But it's like with everything I do, she has to find a way to do it better."

"Don't sweat it, Sarah," Cindy said. "Anybody can stop something from happening."

"Let's go back in," Sarah said. She didn't want anyone to know how upset she was.

"Where were we?" Cindy asked when they walked back into the dining room.

"We've just decided," Jennifer said, "that Kwame and April, being the youngest here—"

"Not fair—" said April.

"—should start the dishes," Jennifer continued, "and Roy has just made a suggestion that sounds cool. If the kids from Hamilton do decide to have a talent contest he can direct it, since he's been in show business."

"I think that's a fantastic idea," Tasha said.

The way Tasha looked at Roy, made Sarah wonder if Tasha wasn't thinking of *him* as one of her special desserts.

47

"And that's my suggestion for tonight," Roy said.

"Then since you've made one suggestion and I've made one, you and I can start the dishes," Sarah said, tossing the notepad she had picked up in the hallway to Kwame.

"Sarah?" Cindy looked at her best friend.

Sarah took Roy's arm and led him into the kitchen. From the other room they could hear Kwame yelling for everyone to slow down as the ideas flew hot and heavy.

"They'll probably come up with a hundred ideas for fund-raising," Roy said.

"Probably," Sarah answered, scraping the dishes over the garbage disposal before stacking them in the dishwasher.

"You and your sister are really something else," Roy said.

"My sister?"

"You and Tasha," Roy said. "Aren't you sisters?"

"Cousins," Sarah answered.

"Then dynamite cousins," he said. "I'd love to take one of you out."

"Oh?" Sarah turned and looked into Roy's eyes. "Which one?"

"You, of course," he said.

Sarah put down the plate she was holding and turned to face Roy. She was mad at Tasha. She was hurting inside. Suddenly this seemed like the right thing to do. She lifted her face to his and kissed him gently, and then again, more passionately.

"I think I picked the right cousin," Roy said when they finally came up for air.

"I think you did, too," Sarah answered. Her heart was beating fast, and she felt as if she was caught in a hurricane. She was scared, angry, hurt, and happy, all at the same time.

"How does Saturday night—dinner and a movie—sound to you?"

"Heavenly," Sarah answered, feeling suddenly terrified but hoping it didn't show. "Just heavenly."

The gang had left and Tasha was sitting crosslegged on the bed playing her guitar when Sarah knocked on the door. "Can I come in?" Sarah asked.

"Why not?" Tasha plucked a few chords and then made a notation on the sheet music lying on the bed in front of her.

"I didn't know you composed," Sarah said, walking over to the bed and looking down at the music. "I'm impressed."

"I'm not very good at it," Tasha said. "But I try."

"You seem to try a lot of things," Sarah said.

"That's my nature," Tasha answered quickly.

"Are you trying to just mess with me, or what?" Sarah asked.

"*Mess* with you?" Tasha threw her head back and laughed.

"You don't know what I'm talking about?" Sarah asked.

"Yeah, I think I know what you're talking about," Tasha said. "You need to control everything that comes near you, and everyone that comes near you. I'm just saying 'no thanks' to being controlled by you."

"You seem to be pretty good at controlling people yourself," Sarah answered. "You seem to have Kwame on a leash."

"Kwame?" Tasha smiled. "He's cute. And I do like him. But if I was looking for a guy I think I'd pick Roy. You know, a man instead of a boy."

"Yeah, I know what you mean," Sarah said, heading for the door.

"Sarah?" Tasha picked up her guitar and played a few chords.

"Yes, cousin dear?"

"Lighten up!"

Sarah closed Tasha's door quietly behind her. The only thing she heard as she went to her room was the fierce pounding of her own heart.

PINE

Six

On Saturday night, Sarah showered and dressed in the bathroom. The black spandex dress she wore fit tightly over her slim figure and was complemented by shimmering tights. She checked herself out in the mirror and nodded in approval. She looked good.

"Sarah, there's a guy downstairs waiting for you!" On the other side of the bathroom door, Allison's voice was breathless.

"Okay," Sarah said as she opened the door. "Tell him I'll be right down."

"It's Roy, the guy—" Allison stopped mid-sentence when she saw her sister. "You eloping or something?"

"No, silly," Sarah laughed. "Just dinner and a movie."

She had told her mother she was going out and playfully ducked her questions about who she was going out with.

"Just be home before the coach turns to a pumpkin, Cinderella," her mother had said.

Most of Sarah's dates, except for dances, had been doubles with Cindy or "semi's" with Kwame. She had explained to her father that a semi was a date with a guy that wasn't exactly a date because it didn't matter that he was a guy. He was a friend to go out with.

"You look awesome." Roy stood when Sarah came down the stairs.

Tasha looked up at her cousin from where she was sitting at the card table, playing chess with Mr. Gordon. "You look very nice," she said, somewhat stiffly.

Sarah smiled, threw her mother a kiss, and headed for the door.

"When do you expect to be home?" Mr. Gordon asked, holding a bishop in his hand.

"Before midnight?" Sarah looked at Roy. He nodded.

"Good," her father answered, putting the bishop down on the board so that it threatened Tasha's queen.

As Roy and Sarah were leaving, Tasha was complaining about how well her uncle played. She showed no sign of being annoyed, but Sarah knew she was. She was a little sorry to realize that that made her happy.

Outside, Roy took Sarah's elbow and directed her toward a sleek black Corvette. "I thought about dinner at Dante's," he said.

"Is this yours?" Sarah asked.

"Legally it belongs to the company I work for," Roy said. "That's convenient for tax purposes."

"Oh." Sarah settled into the bucket seat and waited while Roy went around the back of the car. For a senior this was quite a car, she thought. She hoped she wasn't getting in over her head.

In a moment they were off, Roy handling the stick shift of the two-seater smoothly. Occasional flashes from the streetlights lit up Roy's face, reminding Sarah how handsome he was.

"I really like the way you guys are helping that other school," Roy said. "What's the name of it—Hamilton?"

"Yeah, but we're still disagreeing on how to go about that little task," Sarah said.

"Doesn't matter," Roy said. "You see something that has to be done and you're doing it. In my mind that shows real maturity. Some of the others are nice and everything, but they're still kids. Don't you think so?"

Sarah nodded. She thought over what Tasha had said about Kwame. That he was a boy, while Roy was a man.

"How old are you, anyway?" she asked.

"Eighteen," Roy answered. A few drops of water hit the windshield.

"April said you were managing a group in Detroit."

"It was a small operation," Roy answered. "I wasn't really making that much money. My uncle says that when I graduate he'll help me get into recording."

"Here in Madison?"

"Could be," he said, turning to her. "I see a lot of things in Madison that I like."

Dante's was the best Italian restaurant in Madison. Roy had made reservations but when they arrived the maître d' made them wait. He called a waiter over and spoke to him and the waiter left.

"I don't understand the problem," Roy said, an edge in his voice.

"No problem," was the quick answer.

Another couple came in, who looked as if they might be Italian, and were shown to a table immediately. A moment later the waiter brought two menus over to Sarah and Roy.

"We just thought you would like to check the menu," the waiter said. "It's a courtesy we offer to our new customers."

Roy looked at the menu, and said that it appeared to be fine, and they followed the waiter to a table against the wall.

"What was that all about?" Sarah asked.

"We're black," Roy said. "He just wanted to show us the prices in case we've never eaten in a good restaurant before."

Roy ordered a green salad and the chicken Marsala and Sarah ordered asparagus and prosciutto salad and an entree of pasta with seafood.

"So tell me about yourself," Roy said, when the waiter had taken their orders.

"What would you like to know?" Sarah asked.

"Mostly how you see yourself," Roy said.

"How I see myself?"

"Do you think of yourself as a high school junior almost ready to explore the big wide world, or do you know what you want from life?"

"I know some things that I want," Sarah said. "But I'm still open for new things."

"Well, that certainly sounds intriguing." Roy's voice lowered as he spoke to her. "And what kind of new things are you open for?"

"New experiences, new places," Sarah said.

"You're making Madison sound like a very exciting place," Roy said. "Or is it just that you're very exciting?"

Sarah laughed. "What do you think?" she asked.

"I think you know what I think," Roy said. "I think you know very well what I think."

Sarah took a deep breath. This may be more than I'm ready for, she thought. She decided to play it by ear and see how the evening developed.

The busboy brought bread and water and Sarah

watched as he placed each item carefully on the table. She was thankful for the interruption.

"So, tell me about yourself," she said when the busboy had left.

"Nothing much to tell," Roy said. "I know what I want from life. I want to be creative, to enjoy other creative people, to make enough money to lead the life I want. That's Roy Edwards in a nutshell. How does that sound to you?"

"Sounds fine," Sarah answered.

"I hoped it would," Roy said.

Sarah had heard from Jennifer that the food at Dante's was excellent, and it was. The salad was particularly interesting, with a dressing of a light oil and walnuts that she hoped she would be able to reproduce. She resisted the cart of desserts the waiter brought to their table and settled for a chocolate that came with the bill. She thought about telling Roy that they should petition the school board to have Dante's cater their lunches, and decided to save the joke for the car.

"Thank you for a wonderful dinner," she said as they pulled away from the restaurant.

"Thank you for not once mentioning school," Roy said. "Sometimes when I date young ladies the only thing they talk about is what's happening at school."

"I know what you mean," Sarah said, wondering what he expected her to talk about. She had survived dinner without revealing how nervous she was, and she just wanted the evening to end. Being totally adult wasn't everything she had hoped.

Sarah thought the movie wasn't much. In her opinion, it was the same old plot. Bad guys kill a lot of people. Good guys get mad. Good guys kill a lot of people. Bad guys get even madder.

They were sitting on the side away from the exit in the half filled theater and Roy had his arm around her. She was positive that he was going to try to kiss her and she wasn't sure what she would do.

The movie was almost over when he put his fingers under her chin and turned her face toward his in the darkness. She closed her eyes as their lips touched, first gently and then with more passion. His fingers left her face as he reached across her body and tightly gripped her shoulder. She could feel his arm slide against the front of her body and knew that he was doing it intentionally.

"We're missing the dramatic ending," she said, pulling herself away. This had gone way too far, and she was moving to stop it before it got out of hand.

"I thought we could be the dramatic ending," Roy whispered hoarsely. His hand was on her lap and she took it in her own and held it for the rest of the movie. She decided that holding his hand was better than fighting him off. She was still holding it when the lights came on.

"I think the hero won in the end," Roy said.

"I guess so." Sarah laughed.

The lobby was full of people as they made their way toward the front door.

"Sarah!"

Sarah turned to see José, Billy Turner, and Dave at the popcorn stand.

"Hi, guys!"

"What did you think of the movie?" José asked.

"Same old thing," Sarah said. She saw Dave turn away.

"Nothing wrong with that," José said.

It had grown cooler and the rain slashed against the windshield. The reflections from the neon lights of downtown Madison glistened in the streets.

"Let's go to my uncle's apartment and listen to some music, maybe have some wine..." Roy suggested.

"No thanks. I'd like to go home." Sarah was relieved that the evening was ending.

"Do you have any idea of what you do to me?" Roy asked. "How can you just—"

"Roy, I don't know you that well," she said.

"I thought you knew what you wanted," he responded.

"Right now I'm very tired and I just want to go home," she said.

"Perhaps some other time," he said. He smiled at her.

"Perhaps some other time," she repeated, forcing a smile of her own.

"You know, I don't have an umbrella in the car," he said when they reached her house.

"It's okay, I've been wet before," she said.

"No way I let you get wet again," he said.

He went around to the passenger side of the car, took off his coat, and held it over Sarah as she got out. He wrapped the coat around her as they went to the front door.

"Do you know me well enough to kiss me good-night?" he asked with a smile.

Sarah closed her eyes as Roy kissed her again; then she pushed herself gently away from him.

"Do you want to come in?" she asked, hoping he'd say no.

"No," he said. "I'm tired. Perhaps some other time." Sarah wondered if he was making fun of her.

The living room was dark but there was a light on in the kitchen. Sarah went in and found Miss Essie asleep with her head on the kitchen table. She put her arms around her grandmother and kissed her.

"Huh? What?" Miss Essie awoke and looked at Sarah. "You have a nice time, girl?"

"Wonderful time," Sarah said. "Why aren't you in bed?"

"Wasn't sleepy," Miss Essie said. "Think I'll go up and lie down now, though."

The water in the shower was hot and felt wonderful running down Sarah's body. She had considered telling Miss Essie that she had had an exciting evening, and in a way she had. Going out with Roy was definitely different. He was smooth, and a lot more sophisticated than most boys she knew.

Maybe Roy was right; maybe she did think of herself as just a high school junior and didn't know what she wanted from life. Surely she couldn't have wanted a better dinner, and even the movie hadn't been so bad. She didn't really know Roy at all. Throughout the evening he'd seemed to put different meanings on things than she did.

The shower relaxed her and she was glad to hit the bed. The last thing she thought of before she went to sleep was the lobby of the movie theater. José had called to them and asked if she had liked the movie. Dave had simply turned away. And she did know how she felt about that: terrible.

Seven

Cindy called first thing Sunday, waking Sarah up. It looked to Sarah like everyone else was out.

"So what happened when you went out with him?" Cindy's voice was filled with expectation.

"Nothing," Sarah said. "I think he expected something. At least he acted like he expected something."

"He's got some nerve," Cindy said. "You should have punched him out."

"I guess I came on to him a little," Sarah said. "I'll talk to you about it tomorrow." Sarah felt as if she needed time to collect her thoughts and get this straightened out.

"So did you kiss him or anything?" Cindy went on.

"I don't even want to talk about it," Sarah said. "And yes, I did kiss him."

"Was it a little kiss or...you know?"

"You know *what*?" Sarah said.

"I need details," Cindy said with a smile in her voice. "It's in my blood."

"News now," Sarah said, "details at twelve-fifteen. See you later."

Sarah read the neatly typed note that was taped to the refrigerator door. It was addressed to her and asked her to please rake up the leaves in the front yard. She smiled when she saw "Mommy" typed at the end of the note. She knew who the culprit was.

"Allison!" she called to her sister, but there was no answer.

Mrs. Gordon had obviously told Allison to rake the leaves and Allison was trying to pass it on. It wasn't a big deal, raking leaves, and Allison's note *was* pretty clever. Sarah was headed to the garage to get the rake when the telephone rang. It was Cindy again.

Sarah leaned against the wall and listened. Cindy sounded so upset that Sarah felt sorry for her even though the bad news was about Sarah. Cindy didn't even bother to ask any more questions about Roy. "Don't worry about it," Sarah said. "I'll deal with it. Talk to you later." She hung up the phone, grabbed the rake, and stalked out into the yard.

Most of the leaves in front of the Gordon home

62

had been blown toward the gate and Sarah tackled these first. She worked with a vengeance, but she couldn't get Cindy's words out of her head.

"What she's doing," Cindy had said, "is going around telling everyone that the talent contest is a bad idea. She said you're just trying to control everybody's life."

Sarah would simply have been angry if Cindy hadn't told her that Dave seemed to agree with Tasha. How could Tasha go against her in everything? And how could she do it so successfully? Tasha had a way of getting on people's good side that infuriated Sarah.

She picked up some of the leaves to drop into the trash can, remembered that they had to be put into paper bags for the trash pickup, and threw them down angrily.

"Most people pick leaves up." The boy's voice startled Sarah. "I guess you got something else going for you."

"Oh, I just..." Sarah turned to see an attractive dark-skinned girl and a tall, good-looking white boy. The girl was wearing a pea coat with the collar turned up against the wind. "Can I help you?" Sarah asked.

"We're looking for Mr. Gordon's house," the boy said.

"This is it," Sarah said.

"We're supposed to leave these papers here and pick up some books," the boy said.

63

Sarah didn't remember her father mentioning anyone coming to the house to pick up books. "Well, come on in," she said.

"Nice house," the girl said as they went into the kitchen.

"Who's that?" said Miss Essie, looking around from the stove, where she was making tea. It looked like she'd just woken up. "Cindy? No, that's not Cindy."

"Kiki," the girl said. "Kiki Jones."

"I'm Steve Adams," the boy said. "Kiki's agent."

"Why does she need an agent?" Miss Essie asked, standing over the teapot in her bathrobe.

"I don't," Kiki said. "Don't listen to Steve. We go to Hamilton and we're working on a special project at school today. Mr. Gordon told me to come by and pick up some books," Kiki said. "He asked me because I'm responsible and he told Steve to come along to help carry the books."

"Well, have some tea or juice before you leave," Miss Essie said. She started off toward her room with her tea.

"Did Dad mention anything about any books to you?" Sarah asked.

"No, but I think he was talking to Allison on the phone before she went skating," Miss Essie said.

"You want juice or anything?" Sarah asked when Miss Essie had left.

"Sure," Kiki said. "Mr. Gordon's your dad?"

"Oh, I'm sorry," Sarah said, extending her hand.

"Yes, I'm Sarah Gordon."

"You look like your father," Steve said. He shook Sarah's hand. "But how come you were throwing leaves around the yard? I mean, if that's like a new thing I want to get in on it."

"You're supposed to put the leaves in paper bags," Sarah said. "I forgot and I was going to put them in the trash can."

She put out the juice and a box of cookies that was on top of the refrigerator. Then she went into her father's den to look for the books.

There was a stack of books with a thick rubber band around them. Under the rubber band there was a note that said *Reading Program*. Sarah brought the books into the kitchen.

"Are these the books?" she asked.

Kiki looked at them and nodded. "These are the books."

"Mr. Gordon said that you go to Murphy," Steve said. "How is it?"

"It's the only school I've been to," Sarah said. "I guess it's okay."

"How is it having a principal for a father?" Kiki asked.

"A little rough sometimes." Sarah laughed. "You can't get by with many excuses. On the other hand you can always get help when you need it. How do you like Hamilton?"

"It's okay," Kiki said. Sarah noticed that when Kiki smiled, she was beautiful.

65

"What are you guys going to do with the video equipment when you get it?" Sarah asked.

"We probably won't get it," Steve answered. "We don't count so it probably won't happen. I recommended that we could get the money by selling an English teacher, but they didn't go for it."

"I'd be willing to work for it," Kiki said. "But there aren't that many after school jobs around."

"She thinks she's going to be a television star," Steve said.

"Correction: I *know* I will become a television star," Kiki said.

Sarah remembered what Cindy had told her, that Tasha thought Sarah was trying to control everybody. She decided not to give Kiki too much advice. "You might not be able to get a regular after school job but you could probably get a few odd jobs if people knew you were looking."

"We'd have to get a lot of them," Steve said. "You hear of anything, let us know."

Sarah watched through the front window as Steve and Kiki left. They walked down the street, but then Steve turned and ran back. Sarah thought he was going to come in again but he stopped in the yard, picked up a handful of leaves, and threw them around. He gave Sarah the thumbs up sign and went on down the street.

Sarah went to her room and fell across the bed. She felt bewildered. On the one hand it seemed so right to help the kids at Hamilton get the video equipment. Especially now that she had met Kiki and Steve, it seemed like a good idea. But maybe Tasha was right, she thought. Maybe she did want to control people too much.

She closed her eyes and tried to sort out her feelings. She told herself that what Tasha said didn't matter, but she knew it did. Tasha had moved into her house, into her circle of friends, and even into her innermost feelings. Somehow she felt inadequate around her cousin.

She sat up and looked at herself in the mirror. Her parents told her she had "classic good looks." Everyone thought she was pretty. She felt pretty. But there was something about the way Tasha looked that made her shine. And she didn't seem to ever think about it.

Ideas about getting part-time jobs came into Sarah's mind, and she pushed them out. She started doing her homework, decided that she wasn't in the mood to deal with the influence of Andrew Jackson on the concept of American democracy, and switched on the old black and white television by the bed.

Eight

"Honey?" Sarah felt someone gently shaking her shoulder. She opened her eyes and looked up to see the tall form of her father.

"Hi, Dad, I must have fallen asleep."

"That must have been some boring television program," he said.

Sarah sat up and stretched. "Oh, some kids came by to pick up some books."

"They dropped them by the school," he said. "They were disappointed that we didn't live in a bigger house, but they were impressed by you."

"That Steve is funny," Sarah said.

"Funny and bright," her father said. "He's good at math and he's a computer whiz, but he can't seem to get himself on track. When he does, he'll be ready to transfer to Murphy. By the way, you got a phone call. Roy Edwards left his number."

"Thanks, Daddy."

"Like him a lot?"

"I guess so," Sarah said.

"Did I ever tell you about the time I first dated your mother?" Mr. Gordon asked.

"Forty-'leven times, Dad," Sarah answered.

"Just checking. Finish your homework?"

"Working on it now," Sarah answered.

"In your sleep?" Her father smiled.

"It's a new method invented for American History for when you really can't get into it but know you have to so your father doesn't get on your case," Sarah said.

"Roy's number is next to the phone," her father said before leaving.

Sarah was afraid Roy was going to ask her out again. She hadn't thought a lot about dating in her junior year and when she thought about it she thought of fun, not anything that anybody had to be afraid of. She thought about calling Roy, and then she thought about calling Dave.

What had Cindy said? That Dave seemed to agree with Tasha a lot. Sarah wondered if Dave thought she was trying to control everybody's life.

Tasha's footsteps in the hallway made her tense. She heard her cousin go into her room, and after a few minutes she heard the radio come on. Sarah took a deep breath and went to Tasha's door.

Tasha was lying on the bed reading her French textbook.

"Can I come in?" Sarah asked.

"Why not?" Tasha put the book down.

"Working again," Sarah said. "My, but you do keep yourself busy."

"I try to," Tasha said. "Is there a problem with that?"

"Not as far as I'm concerned," Sarah said. She could feel the tension in her stomach. "I just thought that perhaps you needed some more relaxation in your life."

"Oh?"

Sarah went over to the window seat and sat down. Below the window she could see a few leaves left on the trees in the yard. They were mostly brown, but a few were a brilliant red. She loved the way the leaves changed this time of the year, and how the cycle started again each spring.

"Are you busy tomorrow after school?" Sarah asked.

"Why?"

"I thought that you and I might hang out together for a while. Maybe we could even discuss the talent show."

"I don't think anyone is really that hot for a talent show," Tasha said.

"Don't you mean that *you* are not that hot for a talent show?" Sarah asked.

70

"We can begin with me," Tasha answered quickly. "You're right, I'm not that hot for the talent show. I don't see why we're doing a show for the kids at Hamilton. Well, no, I can see why you want to run the show for Hamilton. I just can't see why the rest of us need to do it."

Sarah blinked in surprise. "Tasha, what's with you? You are just the most contrary person I've ever met!"

"Contrary to what?" Tasha raised her voice. "Contrary to who?"

"To everything and everyone!" Sarah said, feeling the anger rise in her voice. "I was looking forward to your coming. I thought we would be like sisters. I felt sympathy, and friendship toward you. You just seem to feel hostility toward me."

"Sarah, you were looking forward to a victim, which I am not. You were looking forward to a project, something that you could turn into a success. I don't think you can stand the fact that I'm not letting you make a project out of me, so you can show everybody how great you are. That's what you want to do with your Hamilton project, show them how great you are."

"And it's your mission to convince Kwame and Dave that I'm not so great, right?" Sarah stood with her hands on her hips. Tasha was saying things that just weren't true, and Sarah felt hurt.

"It's my mission, as you put it, to be Tasha Gordon," Tasha said. "And I think you're jealous of the attention the guys pay me, especially Dave. I see the way you look at him. I haven't decided if I want him yet. When I make up my mind I'll let you know, though."

Sarah whirled around and stormed out of Tasha's room. The door slammed behind her and she went into her room and slammed her own door.

She had tried to clear the air. She had *tried* to talk to Tasha, but all she had received in return was Tasha's nasty attitude. The girl hated her, that was clear.

"You're not a victim, Tasha," Sarah said to herself. "And neither am I. If you want to bully me about helping the kids at Hamilton, and if you think you want Dave, you'd better be ready for a good fight."

Nine

"Allison, this is not going to work." It was later Sunday afternoon, and Sarah was lying on her bed with her eyes closed.

"It's going to work, believe me." Allison arranged Sarah's arms at her sides.

"It feels like you're laying me out to bury me," Sarah said.

"Just relax and let your mind go completely blank, which shouldn't be too hard for you," Allison said.

"Allison, did I ever tell you you were adopted?" Sarah said.

"Shh. Okay, listen to the sound of my voice..." Allison lowered her voice and moved close to her

73

sister. "You are getting very sleepy. Verrrrrrry sleepy. You want to sleep. You want to sleep more than anything in the world. You are very tired. The only thing you see in your mind are snow white horses running across a misty field. Sleep...sleep..."

"I am sleepy...verrry sleepy," Sarah murmured.

"White horses across a misty field..." Allison said.

"Wait, it's not a misty field," Sarah said. "It's the ocean."

"The ocean?" Allison sat up.

"And the horses are swimming away..."

"Sarah, you are not taking this seriously!" Allison said.

"I am, but I'm not sleepy and I'm not going to go to sleep just because you're putting on a spooky voice," Sarah said.

"You're impossible!" Allison said. "It worked with Tasha. She went right to sleep and dreamed of horses."

"Everything works with Tasha!" Sarah said, opening her eyes.

"Mom said you guys aren't getting along too well," Allison said. "She's letting you settle it yourselves."

"Just what I need," Sarah said, sitting up and crossing her legs in front of her. "Neutrality from my parents."

"Can I borrow a dollar?"

"No."

"I'll tell you who called today."

"Who called for me?"

"Yup. Wait a minute, I'm not sure. A dollar will refresh my memory."

Sarah thought about refusing to bribe her sister. It wasn't the right thing to teach her. Then she thought about who might have called, got a dollar from her drawer, and handed it over.

"Roy Edwards called and asked if you were busy this coming Friday night. I told him no. Then some girl called Kiki called. She left her number. It's on the pad near the telephone."

Sarah had a sinking feeling. Roy had called twice in one day. She knew she didn't have anything to prove to him, or to anybody else, for that matter. And she wasn't afraid of him. At least she thought she wasn't afraid of him. Still, she didn't want to call him.

She went to the kitchen, got a soda from the refrigerator, picked up the note with Kiki's number, and went back to her room. She didn't want to see Tasha. She imagined what Tasha would say if she knew that Roy wanted to see Sarah again and that she was afraid. There, she had admitted it. But why afraid? No, she told herself, she wasn't afraid, just a little nervous. Roy was just too sure of himself, too cocky.

Well, she could be cocky, too. She picked up the phone, found Roy's number on her scratch pad, and dialed it.

"Hello?" Roy's voice was lower on the phone than it was in person.

"Hi!" she said cheerily. "It's Sarah."

"Hey, what's happening?" Roy responded.

"Nothing much," Sarah said. "Trying to get through this homework."

"Now, that's a good schoolgirl for you," Roy said. "Got those important things on your mind."

"I guess so," Sarah said.

"Look, I wanted to know if you want to get together this weekend," Roy said. "Maybe watch some television, order in some Chinese food, get to know each other a little better."

"I'll have to think about it," Sarah said. "My mom wanted me to do something with her this weekend." She knew this was a dumb excuse. But Roy made her feel defensive. She realized that going out with him had been a mistake, and now she was paying the price. She needed to finish this, but she didn't want to be too abrupt.

"I thought you wanted to get to know me better," Roy said. "At least that's what you said last night."

"I do," Sarah said. "I'm just not sure I can make it this weekend."

"Yeah, right." Roy's voice was full of disbelief. "I'll see you in school tomorrow. Maybe by then you'll know what your mama wants you to do with your life. Later."

"So long—" Sarah heard the telephone click off before she finished speaking.

Roy had sounded annoyed and his attitude made Sarah angry—even furious, as she turned on the television. She remembered Kiki's call, and turned the volume down.

There were cartoons on the tube, and Sarah watched as Popeye lay tied to a railroad track. The train was coming but above Popeye, on a tree limb, there was a can of spinach. Good old Popeye. Good old cartoons. They always had the right answer.

She dialed Kiki's number, got Mrs. Jones, told her who she was, and waited for Kiki to come to the phone. While she waited she heard Popeye's theme music in the background on the other end.

"Hello?"

"Kiki, it's Sarah. That spinach fell into Popeye's mouth just in time!"

"Huh? Oh, that's my little brother watching those cartoons. He thinks they put them on just for him," Kiki said. "Can you type?"

"Sure," Sarah said. "I'm not a speed demon but I'm okay."

"We decided to hold an auction to raise the money for the television stuff," Kiki said. "Some of the kids were ready to give up on it and go on using that one raggedy camera we have but Steve and I are pushing

77

for it. We're going to get all sorts of services donated, and then we'll auction them off to raise money."

"Good," Sarah said.

"Anyway—you got Popeye on?" Kiki asked.

"Yes."

"Popeye must really be in love with that girl, as skinny as she is," Kiki said. "Anyway, we're going to make up some forms for people to buy our services on the first weekend in October. If you can type up the forms, make them look good and everything, then maybe we can get the kids here to go along with it."

"I thought they wanted the video equipment," Sarah said.

"Sure they do," Kiki said. "But they're just like everybody else. They want it if it's not too much trouble."

"I know what you mean," Sarah said. "You have the forms you want me to type up?"

"Steve made a pencil copy and I'll get it to your father," Kiki said.

"Great," Sarah answered. "I'll help you all I can."

"Sarah?"

"Yes?"

"You know, of all the teachers at Hamilton, your father is one of the best."

"Thanks," Sarah said. It made her feel good. She hung up the phone, turned up the sound on the television, and pulled a pillow onto her stomach.

78

On the screen Popeye was getting knocked around by Brutus.

At first she thought the noise downstairs was Allison and one of her friends. When it kept up she went to the door of her room and looked out. Tasha came out of her room and looked, too.

"Allison!?" Sarah called out.

"It's me!" called Miss Essie.

Sarah went back to her room and got her juice can and took it downstairs to the kitchen. Tasha had already gone down, taking the stairs two at a time the way she always did.

"I sure don't feel like taking the train all the way into New York City," Miss Essie was saying. "Not in this cold weather."

"Why do you have to go into New York?" Sarah asked.

"She has a reading," Tasha said.

"A what?" Sarah looked at the boxes piled on the table. Miss Essie had done some serious shopping.

"I have to read for this part on some show they're making a pilot for," Miss Essie said. "You know I haven't done that much television work."

"You're going to be on television?" Sarah asked, getting excited. Sarah had always been impressed with the stories of Miss Essie's career as a Broadway actress, but it had been a long time since Miss Essie had done anything but small parts at the local theater.

"I'm just going to read for the part," Miss Essie said. "Jerry Swann called me this morning asking if I would come down. I didn't even know he had my number. Normally, Harriet would call me if there's a reading—Harriet's my agent, Tasha—but I guess I haven't worked professionally in so long he probably forgot I had an agent."

"When did you work last?" Tasha asked.

"What was I in?" Miss Essie squinted and put her chin on her palm. "I remember, it was in that off-Broadway thing. The play was good but it didn't work a bit with that cast."

"Except for you, Miss Essie?" Tasha said.

"I wasn't that good, either," Miss Essie said. "Sometimes when you do a play either the whole cast works or nobody works."

"What's this role?" Sarah asked.

"Jerry said he would send me a script," Miss Essie said. "I asked him if it was a maid's role. I don't play maids."

"You excited?" Sarah asked.

"Excited? Me? Over some little bit part in a pilot that *might* make television?" Miss Essie asked. "Well, I just might be. I just might be."

Sarah kissed her grandmother and then watched as she held up and fussed over the outfits she was thinking of wearing to the reading. Miss Essie's joy made Sarah feel good. She decided to call Cindy.

When Sarah got back to her room there was a battle between superheroes and evil robots on television. She sat down on the edge of the bed and noticed Roy's number on her pad. She circled the number and under it, in neat letters, wrote *EVIL ROBOT.* As she dialed Cindy's number to tell her the good news about Miss Essie, she wondered if Dave ever thought of himself as a superhero.

As usual, Monday came too soon for Sarah. She was leaving her third-period class when she saw a crowd standing around the bulletin board in the hall-way. She saw that they were looking at a newspaper article pinned to the board.

"What's up?" Cindy stood on tiptoes, trying to see over the crowd.

"Some guy from Silver Lake is talking about Dave Hunter in the paper," a voice piped up from the front of the crowd.

The fourth-period bell rang and the crowd dispersed toward their classes. Cindy pushed her way to the bulletin board, and turned quickly away.

"It's about basketball," she said to Sarah. "See you in English."

Sarah got closer to the bulletin board. Even though Cindy was her best friend, she was sorry that she had ever told her about her date with Roy. When Sarah had thought about it later she was sorry she had kissed him in the kitchen. Somehow she had thought she was getting back at Tasha at the time but afterward it had seemed so stupid.

She had been scanning the article, not really

reading it, when she caught sight of Dave's name. She went back and reread the sentence from the beginning.

"They got a pretty good ball player over there named Hunter," Strickland said. "Maybe it's Runter, I don't know. Anyway, I got to go into the Murphy Gym and eat this dude up. Then the scouts will know I'm consistent."

Ten

"What do you think?" Kwame came over to where Sarah was standing. He looked shorter than he usually did and Sarah looked down and saw that he was barefoot.

"Kwame, where are your shoes?"

"I got them soaked in the rain on the way to school," Kwame said. "They're drying out in the chem lab. What do you think of what Strickland said?"

"Who is Strickland?"

"He's this guy who plays for Silver Lake. All the big colleges are trying to recruit him. He hurt his knee at the end of last season and now all the scouts want to see if he's okay. He figures if he messes over

Dave he'll be a big man."

"He can't just 'mess over' Dave," Sarah said confidently.

"I don't know about that," Kwame said. "A lot of people say he's pro material. And if he really shows Dave up it's going to hurt Dave's chance to get a scholarship."

"Dave is good," Sarah said. "I think he'll be okay."

"Anyway, Tasha is helping him get ready for the game tomorrow," Kwame said, backing away from Sarah. "Gotta go get some learning."

Sarah felt her face burn. How did Tasha always manage to get herself involved in everything? She couldn't imagine Dave needing Tasha's help in basketball.

She was late for English and answered Mrs. Bender's glance with an embarrassed shrug. The period raced by with Sarah thinking about Tasha and Dave on the basketball court. That was how things worked in the movies. The girl was cute as anything but turned out to be a great athlete and everybody was shocked. That kind of movie always ended with the guy falling for the girl.

Roy Edwards was in her math class. He sat in the back. Each time she turned around he was looking at her. He wasn't smiling, just looking at her as if his seriousness was supposed to mean something.

Sarah told herself that she didn't care how Roy Edwards was looking. She just didn't like him. And as for Dave, she had known him all her life and wasn't interested in him romantically.

She wrote Dave's name down and her name under it. She drew a circle around Dave's name and went over it slowly, making the circle slightly smaller each time, until the name had nearly disappeared.

Mr. Cala was talking about how the ancient Egyptians used triangles to build the pyramids, and Sarah imagined thousands of brown-skinned men looking at some guy wearing a bath towel and using a plastic triangle to figure out how high the pyramids should be.

Her thoughts were interrupted when a note landed in the middle of her desk. She opened it, already knowing that it was from Roy. It told her to meet him in the auditorium when the class was over. She crumpled the paper in her hand and dropped it into her backpack.

"Miss Gordon, do you think you might like to join us?" Mr. Cala sat on the edge of his desk.

"I'm listening!" Sarah said.

"Then was the answer A or B?" the teacher asked.

"B," Sarah said, trying to sound confident.

"There was no question, Miss Gordon," Mr. Cala said. "Now try to pay attention."

Math ended with Mr. Cala passing out a short quiz that he wanted the class to do at home.

"Give yourself exactly fifteen minutes to finish the test," he said over the shuffle of feet as the class headed for the door. "And don't cheat. I want you to get used to taking timed tests."

Roy was waiting in the last row of the auditorium when Sarah arrived. She sat on the arm of one of the seats.

"Well?" she said, looking at him and wishing she hadn't come.

"Hey, I'm glad you could make it," Roy said. "Look, we're not getting our relationship off to a great start. So when can we try it again?"

"I don't know," Sarah said. She wondered if they were even *having* a relationship. They weren't as far as she was concerned.

"You're not afraid of going out with me, are you?" His smile was bright and even.

"Of course not," Sarah said.

"This weekend?" he said. "Maybe we can lighten it up a little. A little bowling or something, okay?"

"Yeah, maybe," Sarah said, taking up her backpack. "I gotta go. I was already late for homeroom."

PINE

Eleven

The school was buzzing over the article about Dave. By noon Strickland was being talked about as if he were already a professional, and by three he was a legend.

There was some talk that Dave was nervous and was working out with Tasha in the gym. Sarah went to the gym after school and watched the team work out. Tasha was there in her sweats taking notes.

Sarah needed to think. Tasha was stealing Dave, Roy couldn't take a hint—everything was a mess. She decided a long walk might help.

It had stopped raining and there were huge puddles along 17th Street. Sarah turned down Pine, started into 18 Pine, then changed her mind.

By the time she made it home she was exhausted. An oil truck had splashed her on her long walk, and she went into the bathroom, kicked off her shoes, and washed her legs. She wondered if the driver had splashed her on purpose.

There were carrots in the refrigerator. One good thing about Tasha was that she had introduced them all to fresh veggies.

Sarah peeled two carrots, started to pour some apple juice, and noticed that the container was only a third full. She put the apple juice under one arm, and a box of Fig Newtons under the other, put the carrots in a glass, and headed for her room.

The phone rang as she reached the second floor. She put everything down on the bed, caught the juice just as it started to spill, and answered the phone. It was Kiki Jones.

"How are you?" Sarah asked, bringing the phone cord over her head so that she could lie on the bed.

"All right." Kiki's voice on the phone was punctuated by the sounds of her chewing gum. "I don't know if the auction is going to fly. We can't get any publicity," she said. "Nobody cares. And without publicity, no one will come. We're stuck."

"Who did you go to?" Sarah asked.

"We called the newspaper," Kiki answered. "And they said it wasn't news. Then we went down to the office and asked what they could do and they gave us this long story which ended up being a lot about nothing."

"I know what you mean," Sarah said.

"How're you doing?" Kiki asked.

"You ever have one of those days where nothing goes right?" Sarah asked.

"I think I'm having one of them, too," Kiki said with a sigh. "Have you got any ideas about how we can get word around about the auction?"

"A few," Sarah said.

"I figured if you were anything like your father you'd come up with something," Kiki said. "That's the way he is."

"Kiki, can you come over tomorrow?" Sarah asked.

"Can't," Kiki said. "I have to watch my little brother. I'll give you a call, though."

"Okay, make it late, there's a basketball game tomorrow."

"Some of our guys are going to watch it," Kiki said. "They want to see this guy from Silver Lake. I hope Murphy wins."

Sarah thought Kiki had sounded sincere. She really wanted the auction to work. Sarah had just one idea, and she wasn't sure if that was going to work. She thought for a while and then called the Madison newspaper and asked for the sports desk.

PINE

Twelve

"Looks like all of Silver Lake must be here," Kwame said as he settled down next to Jennifer and Sarah. "And this isn't even a league game."

"Which one is Strickland?" Jennifer looked down at the gym floor, where the players from both teams were finishing their warm-ups.

"That's him talking to the cheerleaders," Kwame said.

Sarah looked at Strickland and then over at Dave. From where she sat she couldn't tell which of them was taller.

"What was Tasha helping him with?" she asked, trying to make her question seem casual.

"Something about what foot he was taking off

90

from when he shot his jumper," Kwame said.

"I didn't like that Strickland talking about how he had to show Dave up," Jennifer said.

"Did you see their cheerleaders?" Kwame peered over the top of his glasses. "Definitely classy."

"I think they're truly unique," Jennifer said. "I mean, if you really go for ugly and awkward."

"I love an objective opinion," Kwame said.

Sarah watched as the Murphy Marauders took their final shots and went to the far bench. Dave sat and the team stood around him. In the stands behind the benches the fans who had come to root for Silver Lake waved small brown and blue pennants and cheered for Strickland. The tension was mounting.

Strickland might be a big deal, but Sarah knew that Dave was hoping that basketball would help him to get into college, too. With his grade point average he could go to any school he wanted but he'd need scholarship money.

Sarah watched as the Silver Lake cheerleaders started a formation that quieted their fans down. They broke into a cheer that didn't seem particularly well done and Jennifer nudged her. The refs took a ball to mid-court and the teams started onto the court.

Jennifer held up her crossed fingers and Sarah crossed hers just as she spotted Roy Edwards coming toward her.

Roy sat next to her as the ref tossed the ball into the air. Sarah smiled without turning to him, keeping her eyes on the game.

Strickland got the ball and dribbled down the sideline, switching hands as he crossed to the top of the key. Dave was guarding him loosely. Suddenly Strickland pointed toward a spot on the floor behind Dave, faked toward it, and then pulled up for a jump shot.

Dave turned quickly, screening Strickland from a possible rebound, but the ball dropped cleanly through the net and the Silver Lake crowd roared.

When Murphy High had the ball it seemed that everyone took a shot except Dave. When Silver Lake got the ball Strickland controlled it. He looked stronger than Dave, forcing his way to the basket for easy lay-ups or sometimes making a spectacular dunk at the end of a fast break.

Strickland was strong but Dave seemed smooth. Once he came down the court and Strickland streaked across the floor to stop him at the foul line. Dave faked left but moved quickly to his right with a long graceful glide, his dark body slanting away from the defender even while the ball went behind his back to the waiting hands of José. Then José laid the ball up softly against the glass backboard even as Strickland, unaware that the ball had been passed, tried to reach around Dave to stop him.

"Yes! Yes!" Kwame screamed his approval down to the floor.

"All right!" Roy shouted. He had put his arm around Sarah's shoulder and rocked her toward him.

The score was close, but Dave had only scored one basket while Strickland was doing everything for Silver Lake. On one play Strickland and Dave were under the basket. A pass came in to Strickland and he went high into the air. Dave went up with him but Strickland just slammed the ball through the hoop with one hand.

"You're looking good," Roy whispered into her ear. "I'd like to go one on one with you."

Sarah smiled weakly.

"Is that a yes or a no?" Roy asked.

Sarah shrugged and leaned forward to move away from his arm.

At halftime Silver Lake was ahead, 25 to 33. Dave had played most of the first half and he hadn't looked that good to Sarah. Roy bought her a soda and Jennifer started talking about how she thought the cheerleaders from Silver Lake were tacky.

"Just what do you mean by tacky?" Sarah asked.

"Like, lacking in a sense of color," Jennifer said.

"Those are probably their school colors," Kwame said.

"Then they should have had the good taste to go to another school," Jennifer sneered.

Sarah felt miserable, for herself and for Dave. She wanted to go down to the locker room and tell him how much she was rooting for him.

When the teams came out for the second half Sarah could see Tasha sitting behind Murphy's team. She was smiling and looking really cheerful. She

93

didn't even seem to care that they were losing by eight points.

"Okay!" shouted Kwame as the teams came back on the court.

Sarah had all her fingers crossed as the game resumed.

Strickland made a move on Dave, who stripped the ball from him and threw it all the way down the court to Glenn Peters. Glenn grabbed it and made a spinning reverse lay-up over a straining Silver Lake player to bring the Marauders within six points of Silver Lake.

The game continued with each Murphy score answered by Silver Lake. Dave was looking better. Strickland blocked two of his shots in a row, but he made the third and managed to knock the ball out of Strickland's hands once. Even though Strickland got the ball back it was clear that he was annoyed.

Strickland got his revenge by scoring three quick baskets, which quieted the Murphy crowd.

A Murphy player was fouled and made both shots.

"Hey, we're still in it," Roy said. He put his hand on Sarah's knee. "How you doing, baby?"

"Not too good," Sarah answered. "I think it's the heat. I'm going to the ladies room."

"Hurry back, baby," Roy said as Sarah went past him to the aisle.

By the time Sarah reached the hallway outside the

gym her eyes were already filled with tears. She started to walk, then ran down the hall to the first-floor bathroom.

She splashed her face with water and told herself she was being foolish. But the tears, foolish or not, still came and she banged her fist against the sink in frustration. Why did she have to feel like this, she asked herself. Why?

The door opened and she turned away quickly.

"Sarah?" It was Tasha.

Sarah turned on the water full force and put her head down.

"Are you okay?" Tasha asked.

Sarah looked at her cousin, trying desperately to keep her composure. She felt her lip quiver. "I'm okay," she heard herself saying through clenched teeth. "Just leave me alone!"

Tasha looked at her, shrugged, and turned away. She went to the door, put her hand on the knob, and then turned back toward Sarah.

"Sarah, you're not okay," she said, softly. "What's wrong?"

"Everything, I guess," Sarah said. "Just everything you said is coming true. I wanted to do something for the kids at Hamilton and I think I just blew it for them. I told them that I could get one of the sports writers to put something in the paper about their auction. Then I called the paper and they said that it just wasn't news. Then I came to the game to see..."

"To see Dave?" Tasha put her hand on Sarah's wrist.

"No, not really." Sarah looked away.

"Yes, really," Tasha said. "He told me how special he feels you are."

"He said that?" The cheers from the basketball game filtered through the door. They seemed ever so far away.

"You didn't know how he felt about you?"

"Tasha, I don't know what's going on in my life anymore," Sarah said. "I just know that nothing is working out right. I just wanted to come here today and root my dumb head off for Dave and instead of that I'm sitting up there with Roy trying to make a move on me."

"Hey, I'm not helping either, am I?" Tasha took a paper towel and started wiping Sarah's face.

"Not exactly," Sarah said, trying to smile through her tears.

"Look, you're too upset to go back to the game, and I don't think you want to see Roy anymore today," Tasha said. "Why don't you go on home and I'll bring the gang by later. We can do some serious girl talking tonight. I'd start now but I have to get my nerve up before I tell you how afraid of you I was when I got here."

"Afraid of me?"

"I'll tell you more about it later," Tasha said. "Right now I have to see how your guy is doing."

"He's not my guy yet," Sarah said.

96

"We can work on that, too," Tasha said. "See you later."

Sarah went directly home and fell across the bed. She couldn't remember doing that much, but she was exhausted and was soon asleep. The next thing she knew, she was hearing voices downstairs. She wiped her face with a Kleenex and went out into the hall.

"Hello?" she called out.

"Sarah, we're back from the game," called Tasha.

"Be right down," Sarah answered and went down the stairs to the kitchen.

"We thought we'd come here instead of 18 Pine. I'm going to make some of my famous jalapeño chips and dip," Kwame said as he emptied a bag of fixings onto the counter.

"I'm sorry I missed the end of the game but I had to get home to work on something," Sarah said, glancing toward Tasha.

"No sweat. You didn't miss much. We lost by twelve points." Dave was leaning against the counter.

"I think the guys did fine. And with Gene out with the flu I think they did a lot better than expected." Kwame punctuated his speech with vigorous waves of a cheese-covered wooden spoon.

"Hey, watch it." Billy Turner moved away, wiping some cheese sauce from his cheek.

"Dave came on strong at the end," Tasha said.

"He had twelve points and nine assists."

"Didn't touch Strickland, though," Dave said. "Did you see those scouts watching him?"

"They all came to see him but they still got a look at other guys, too. Namely you." Tasha poked her finger into Dave's chest.

"You really think so?" asked Cindy.

"They can't all have Strickland. It's their job to be out there to find the good stuff. And we at Murphy have the goods." Kwame put out two large trays of corn chips covered with cheese.

"Kwame, that stuff is going to rot your gut out!" Cindy said.

"That smells good." Mr. Gordon came through the kitchen door. "How did it go, Dave?"

"We lost but we've got another game with them next month," Dave said. "We'll see what happens then."

"Once you play a team—" Mr. Gordon was interrupted by the ringing of the phone. "Hello?" He picked up the phone with his right hand and reached for the dip with his left. "Speaking."

There was a long silence. Then Mr. Gordon answered the caller in a subdued voice. Finally, he hung up.

"That was Carl Parrish," Mr. Gordon announced. "He says Steve has been picked up by the police on an auto theft charge. Parrish was almost gloating. I'm sure he's going to try to use this to call the auction off."

"He can't do that," Tasha said. "He has no right to blame all the kids at Hamilton for what one kid does."

"Steve is a good kid," Mr. Gordon said. "I don't know if he's done anything. I'm going into the other room to call the police. He may need some help."

"Steve is that white kid from Hamilton, right?" Kwame asked. "The one who might transfer to Murphy?"

"Right," Sarah said.

"Why did he have to steal a car now?" Kwame asked.

"Why do you have to assume he's guilty?" Tasha asked.

"Okay, maybe he's not guilty," Kwame said. "In that case we'll only give him ten years."

Mr. Gordon came back into the kitchen, pulling up the zipper on his parka.

"I hope it's not too serious," he said. "Something about driving without a license. He's already been released to his parents."

"And it doesn't matter if they try to stop the auction anyway," Cindy said. "They don't have to do it as a school function."

"No, that just won't do. It has to be done as a school function or not at all," Mr. Gordon said. "You can't ask people to donate and participate in a benefit for the school if the school wants no part in it. And you can bet your bottom dollar that Carl Parrish is going to try to get the school board to stop the auction."

"Maybe we can talk to the board," Tasha said.

"Yeah, that's right. Mr. Parrish isn't the whole school board," Dave said.

"Even if he does have the biggest mouth." Cindy beat out Billy for the last chip on the plate.

"We'll see," Mr. Gordon said. "Tell your mother I'll see her later. I want to get the story straight from Steve."

Mr. Gordon left and Kwame said he had to go, too.

"You ingrates want to help clean up?" Tasha asked.

There was a chorus of no's followed by a quick gathering of books, sneakers, and backpacks as Sarah and Tasha were abandoned in the Gordon kitchen.

Thirteen

"You want to learn some guitar chords?" Tasha asked. She took the guitar out of the closet and laid it across the bed.

"Not really," Sarah said. "Like, maybe I do, but I'm not sure...I don't see myself touring with Prince this year." Sarah's head still ached from all the excitement at the basketball game.

"Sarah, when I came here you thought I had a chip on my shoulder, didn't you?" Tasha said.

"I wanted to be helpful and I pushed it too much," Sarah said. "I'm really sorry."

"I did have a chip," Tasha said. "Uncle Donald seemed so nice and everything and your mom is like right out of *The Ladies' Home Journal* or something. My dad always said that his brother was something like that…you know…perfect teeth, and real nice. No warts, no big mistakes."

"Dad's okay."

"No, he's better than that. He's really cool. He cares about people and he's just a neat guy. And all my life I've been hanging around athletes, and traveling from city to city."

"It must have been fun," Sarah said.

"Yeah, I guess it was. But I never really got to know my dad. He was never home. All I ever got to know about him was what Mom talked about. Can you understand that?"

"I guess so." Sarah took off her sneakers and found a blister on her toe.

"Didn't that hurt?" Tasha asked. "I mean, your toe must have been really painful."

"Everything's been a pain today," Sarah said. She rubbed her foot. "I thought you hung out with your dad a lot. You're a good athlete and everything."

"Hung out with him?" Tasha picked up the guitar and put it across her lap. "I used to read the sports pages every day so that I would know everything about sports. I used to read every football biography I could. First I would read about something, then I would say that my father told it all to me."

"So when you came here with Dad…"

"I knew you had a good relationship with your parents—"

"And I'm sure that your father loved you as much

102

as Dad loves me—as much as Dad loves you," Sarah said.

"Maybe." Tasha smiled and Sarah saw that her eyes were glistening. "I kind of think he did. I just wish we had had more time together. And Sarah, I'm really sorry I treated you so mean. One thing I did get from my father is how to compete."

"It's no big deal," Sarah said.

"Thanks, I needed that." Tasha moved her fingers slowly across the guitar strings. "And now, on to our next topic. What are you doing with Mr. Roy Edwards?"

"What do you think I'm doing?" Sarah asked.

"I think you're getting in over your head," Tasha said. "Swimming with the sharks."

"He's a creep." Sarah had both of her socks off and was massaging her toes. "He's like a smooth creep, but still a creep. He was trying to come on to me during the game. I'm worried about our team and he's trying to set up a rendezvous."

"That's what some guys are like," Tasha said. "What they do is grab and grope and gab and hope."

"You've got Roy down to a T," Sarah said.

"I know his type," Tasha said. "I went out with this guy last year—"

"You have a lot of dates?"

"Mostly we used to go out with a group," Tasha said. "Nothing heavy. Anyway, his father had a Benz and he thought he was pretty hot stuff. Once he asked me to come over to his house to study and he

103

had this record on and it was supposed to have a hidden message."

"And this hidden message was supposed to make you fall madly in love." Sarah lay on the floor and put her legs up on Tasha's bed.

"Right, only I couldn't hear it and he got mad and called me stupid." Tasha dragged her fingers across the guitar strings. "And his idea of a fabulous date was him telling me how wonderful he was, how stupid I was, playing that silly record, and reaching for my various parts. All at the same time."

"Gross!"

"This fool was a step beyond the ultra max, but..." Tasha said, smiling, "he had the coolest wheels in town."

"I'm tired," Sarah said, getting up. "I'm really tired but I'm happy, too. Gotta grab some sack time."

"We'll get our strategy together in the morning," Tasha said.

"To get the auction going again?" Sarah asked.

"Get the auction going, defuse Roy, conquer the world...who knows?"

"Tasha, now that we're friends, can I ask you a question?"

"Sure, go on."

"Are you available for occasional hugs?" Sarah asked.

"Yeah, I think so."

Sarah went to the edge of the bed and put her

arms around Tasha. She didn't want to seem too mushy, and she certainly didn't want to cry again. As she left she heard Tasha playing slow chords on the guitar.

PINE

Fourteen

Sarah stood on the high stage, a microphone in one hand, and looked out over the huge audience. She started her song, but as soon as she did the audience began to laugh. She stopped, determined to run off the stage. The audience stopped laughing and she looked closer. Puppies! She was facing an audience of puppies. She started to sing again, and again they started to laugh! She began to run, but something was holding her back, something tangled around her legs...

Sarah twisted in her bed and finally succeeded in kicking her way out of the covers. She sat straight up. What a weird dream! Then she heard it again, the sound of a crowd laughing. She slipped out of bed, grabbed her robe, and opened the door to her room. She heard the laughter again. Then she heard Miss Essie's voice.

Sarah made a quick trip into the bathroom to splash water on her face and then headed downstairs.

"Morning, baby." Mrs. Gordon was putting the pitcher of orange juice on the table. Miss Essie was standing near the cupboard drinking coffee, Sarah's father was sitting at his usual place, and Allison was half asleep over a bowl of cereal.

"What's that laughter?" Sarah asked, noticing the tape recorder on the table next to the toast.

"That's what I have to put up with!" Miss Essie said.

"Your grandmother was offered the part in the new television show," Mr. Gordon said, smiling. "She's not sure about the canned laughter, though."

"The program is done in a studio," Miss Essie said. "But they want to give the impression it's being done before a live audience so they have this canned laughter and every time you say something that's supposed to be funny the engineer adds in this laughter. Go on, say something funny."

"Like what?" Sarah asked.

The moment she finished talking Miss Essie pushed the "play" button on the tape recorder and a peal of laughter came through the speakers. Sarah smiled.

"I'm used to the live stage. Working in a quiet studio is—" Miss Essie paused.

"It's strange," Sarah said. "But getting a part on the program is great. Are you going to take it?"

"I don't know," Miss Essie said.

"But she has been smiling since she heard the good news last night," Sarah's mother poured a glass of juice and pushed it in front of her elder daughter. "Heard Murphy lost the game last night. That's too bad."

"It was close, though," Allison said, her head still down on the table.

"Any more ideas about Steve Adams?" Sarah asked her father.

"I got a call from one of the board members this morning," he said. "She asked me if I was going to continue 'being difficult.'"

"And what did you say?" Sarah asked.

"What do you think he said?" Miss Essie asked. "He said he was going to support his kids!"

"And then she said that there'd be trouble," Mr. Gordon said.

"And you said…?" Sarah looked at her father.

"He said…" Allison reached over and punched the tape recorder and the whole family joined the recorded laughter.

"Look, I've got to get out of here," Mr. Gordon said. "But believe me, it's not going to be as easy as all that. I'm afraid that if the board is against the kids raising their own funds I'm going to have to back off."

Mr. Gordon left just as Allison was letting the

milk spill over onto the table.

"You've got one good daughter, Dad," Sarah called after him.

"Make that two!" Tasha came down to breakfast as cheery as usual. Sarah told them all about her dream. Everybody was interested in the way the laughter came into her dream.

Everybody except Allison. "What kind of puppies were they?" she asked.

"I don't know," Sarah said, "just puppies."

"It was your dream. You should know what kind they were," Allison insisted.

"I'm late for school," Sarah said, standing.

"If you guys get home early see what you can do about the drain in the sink downstairs," Mrs. Gordon said. "I think there's something stuck in it."

"We may be late," Tasha said. "I think we're going to have to call a strategy meeting."

"Just don't do anything that's going to work against the kids," Mrs. Gordon said.

The day was as bright and crisp as Sarah's mood. Each time she saw Tasha during the day she had to smile, and it was making her feel a bit silly. Tasha was going to think she had a canned smile, the way Miss Essie's television show had canned laughter. Before going to school that morning Sarah had called Kiki Jones and asked her to come to 18 Pine in the afternoon.

"What I'm not going to do," Sarah told Cindy, "is to take charge of everything the way I usually do.

I'm going to listen to everybody's opinion."

"I think we should get up a petition," Cindy offered. "That way—"

"No way," Sarah said. "That's not strong enough. Mr. Parrish would just say that it was juvenile."

"Well." Cindy smiled. "As long as you're going to listen to everybody's opinion."

It was 3:40 when Sarah edged into the corner booth at 18 Pine. Kwame, Cindy, Jennifer, and April were already dividing a medium pizza. In a moment Sarah saw Kiki Jones open the door. Sarah stood up and waved her over.

"Hey, Sarah," Kiki greeted her as she looked at the faces around the table.

"I hope you can stand mushrooms," Kwame said. "Cindy says they're good for your skin. I've seen the skin on these suckers and I hope they don't do me like that."

"Kiki, this is Cindy, this is April, and this is Jennifer," Sarah said, pointing to her friends. "And the mouth under the glasses belongs to Kwame."

"Hi." Kiki's smile was instantly friendly. "Steve wasn't in school today," she told them. "I called but his father said he couldn't come to the phone." Kiki sat down in Sarah's seat next to Jennifer. "Things don't look too good. Maybe we should wait a while for the auction."

"Why? No one's done anything except maybe Steve and we don't really know about that," Sarah said.

110

"Well, you know how adults are," Kiki said. "If they think they're taking a chance they back right off. And I don't think Steve did anything wrong, but you know he's got this reputation as being...you know...a little flaky."

"He ever mess with somebody's car before?" Kwame asked.

"No, but one time we all went down to the mall and he started dancing with one of the dummies—"

"Whoa!" April spit out a mouthful of soda. "Steve was the one that did that? I heard about that. He took the dummy from the floor and danced with it up the escalator, right?"

"Something like that." Kiki grinned.

"We have big trouble," Jennifer said. "You know that this dude you're talking about—what's his name?"

"Mr. Parrish," Sarah said.

"You know he's going to bring up the mall bit," Jennifer said.

"Here comes Tasha." Kwame pointed toward the door with his chin.

Sarah introduced Tasha to Kiki, and April filled Tasha in on Steve's reputation.

"But that's mostly our problem," Kiki said. "We get reputations as either bad kids or kids who aren't serious and then we have to live with that the rest of our lives."

"Yeah, but dancing with a dummy is a little far-out," Kwame said.

"Kwame, do you remember that dance we had last year in school?" Jennifer asked. "When all the girls had dance cards?"

"Sure, all the parents were checking out how close we were dancing," Kwame said.

"Right," Jennifer said. "And speaking of dancing with dummies, I think a lot of us danced with you."

"Ouch!" Tasha winced as Kwame grabbed his chest in mock pain.

"Kiki's right," Sarah said. "Steve's reputation will hurt us. We need to come up with a strategy that doesn't depend on Steve being somebody's angel."

"I still think it's a great idea," Tasha said. "Auctioning off the services of the kids seems just perfect."

"Steve's idea," Kiki said.

"Maybe that's it," Sarah said. "The basic idea is kids doing something for themselves. And what are adults always running their mouths about?"

"April!" April made a stern face and lowered her voice as she imitated her father. "Can't you ever do anything for yourself?"

"That sounds a little bit like my mother," Kwame said. "If it was my father the language would have been a lot spicier."

"Sarah's right, we can use that," Tasha said. "We just have to figure how."

"It had better be soon, too," Kiki said. "The kids at Hamilton are getting pretty discouraged."

Sarah walked Kiki to the bus stop and waited with

her until the bus came. Kiki had said that the other kids at Hamilton were getting discouraged, but Sarah saw that she was discouraged, too.

"I don't know why I feel so bad when people turn me down for something," Kiki said. "I hate asking people for things and they keep saying no."

"I know what you mean," Sarah said.

"Do you?" Kiki turned toward Sarah quickly. Then the inquisitive look on her face softened to a smile.

"This your bus?" Sarah asked as the Number 10 pulled to the curb.

"This is it," Kiki said. She was smiling again. "See you later, girlfriend."

Sarah had flushed slightly when Kiki asked her if she really understood how it felt to be turned down for something. Sarah hadn't been turned down for much in her life. She had all the important things and she knew it. As she headed down Pine she wondered what Kiki's life was like, or Steve's for that matter.

The beep of a car horn interrupted her thoughts. It was Roy Edwards. "Hey, girl, need a lift?"

Sarah could have used the time to think on the walk home but didn't know how to put Roy off. He pushed open the door and she got in next to him.

"Looked like you were in another world," Roy said. "I honked three times."

"I was thinking. You know that auction we were planning with the kids from Hamilton? It looks like

113

we may have to call it off. Or it may be called off no matter what we want."

"How come?"

"One of the kids we're working with from Hamilton, Steve Adams, got picked up last night. At first the rumor was that he stole a car. Then it was just that he was driving it without a license. But it might not matter what he did at this point. This guy on the school board is against the auction and he's going to make a big deal out of it, I'm sure."

"That's too bad. But why don't you guys go ahead and have it without their help? It's a free country."

"Mom and Dad say it's got to be a school function or nothing. So unless we get the school board's okay, that's it." Sarah was glad to see the corner of her block coming up.

"Look, I've got a cousin who's a big-deal public relations guy at Shields & Hoffman," Roy said. "You know the company?"

"No," Sarah answered.

"They do a lot of work with the community and I could talk to him. I think he mentioned something about knowing people on the school board." Roy stopped the car three houses down from Sarah's. "Look, I know our first date wasn't the greatest but I think we ought to take another shot at it. How about dinner and whatever on Friday? We could stop at my cousin's before we go."

"I'd like to talk with your cousin but let's keep the dating thing separate, okay?"

"You giving me the cold shoulder, baby?" Roy turned his head toward Sarah and then away.

"Let's just keep one thing separate from the other," Sarah said.

"So you want to go out Friday or not?" Roy asked.

"I think not," Sarah said, holding her breath. She still didn't know why she was so tense around Roy.

"Okay, no hurry," Roy said, reaching across her lap and pushing open the door. "Call me when you're ready for the date. I wouldn't want to rush you or anything. Then we'll set up something with my cousin."

"Yeah," Sarah opened the door and got out. "You just wait for my call."

By the time Sarah reached the gate, Roy's car had passed by with a beep and she was racing up the stairs with her cheeks burning. She wasn't hurt, but so mad she could feel tears starting to form in her eyes. She opened the door and ran right up to her room, ignoring Allison who was in the kitchen.

How could she have even gone out with that sleaze in the first place? All he seemed to care about was himself. Sarah wanted to talk to Cindy. She wanted to talk to everybody, to her mother, to Miss Essie, to the whole world. But sometimes there were things you could only say to people you had talked to before. People who you knew would lend a sympathetic ear.

She reached for the phone and dialed her best

friend's number. The ring sounded five times and Sarah knew Cindy wasn't home. She usually got the phone on the third ring even if she was in the cellar.

As soon as she hung up the receiver the phone rang, and she picked up before the ring had finished.

"Sarah, don't you think wearing black will make me look sophisticated?" It was April. "Cindy is here helping me pick out an outfit for my aunt's engagement party."

"I don't know, April. Let me talk to Cindy." Sarah was relieved to hear her friend's voice. "Cindy, I was trying to reach you."

"I went home with April. What's up?"

"I've got to talk to you. But not on the phone. It's really important."

"You want to come over here to April's or what?"

"I'll come over. See you in a few minutes."

"Enter the winter residence of the Winters." Cindy curtsied as she opened the front door of April's house. The house was done in light shades of beige and a lot of white. It looked like a good idea gone bad. But the upstairs, where there were three bedrooms off a neatly decorated hall, seemed comfortable in an old-fashioned way.

There were dresses all over April's bed and April herself was dressed in what the fashion magazines called "a little black dress." On April it looked like a big black dress. It was much too long and the top was too big. The shoulder pads hung down on the

116

tops of her arms, leaving her own narrow shoulders to hold up the rest of the dress.

"It belonged to mom number two," April said. April's father had remarried twice after his divorce from her mother.

"I don't think I can fix this dress so it'll look like anything," Cindy said. "And even if I did she just looks dead in that flat black."

"You could use some color." Sarah agreed. She sat crosslegged on the floor while Cindy sat in the rocking chair and tucked her legs under her.

"You sounded a little glum on the phone," Cindy said, glancing at April.

"I need an objective opinion about something." Sarah looked at them both. April had flopped on the bed on top of the dresses. "I was walking home this afternoon from the bus stop when Roy Edwards came by. He was driving that same black Corvette and he asked me if I wanted a lift. So I got in…"

"You said you didn't…" began Cindy.

"Hold on and let me finish. I didn't really want to get in but, you know…"

"No, I don't know," Cindy said.

"Well, I didn't know what to say and anyway I wasn't that far from home. Anyway he asked me what I was thinking about and I told him about that thing with Steve, the auction and the school board. Then he offers to help us. And he says we can do it when I go to dinner and whatever with him. And I should call him when I'm ready to go out with him."

Phew! Slimy!" April squealed.

"That weasel!" Cindy put her feet on the floor and leaned forward. "What did you say?"

"I was really mad. I said for him to just wait for me to call."

"What did he say?" April asked.

"Nothing. He just let me out like nothing had happened and waved as he drove off."

"Who does this fool think he is?" Cindy's voice was quiet.

"Did he really say it like that?" April asked. "I mean, if you go out with him—"

"And *whatever*," Cindy added.

"I told it to you just as it happened and you had the same reaction as I did. I even said to leave the dating thing out of it and then he said I should call him when I was ready for the date." Sarah looked from the wide brown eyes of her best friend to April's even wider blue eyes.

"Look, do you like Roy?" Cindy said.

"No way." Sarah shook her head.

"Then you shouldn't date him," April sat up and started taking off the dress. "And you shouldn't even take a ride with him."

"You should be dating Dave," Cindy said.

"But Dave hasn't asked me." Sarah put her knees up in front of her and hugged them to her chest.

"If he did, what would you say?" Cindy said.

"He hasn't been too friendly, lately."

"What would you say?" Cindy repeated.

"I'd say yes. In a minute."

"Exactly." Cindy stood up like a lawyer who had just proved her case. "So since you want to go out on a date with him, and you would say yes if he asked you, then ask him."

PINE

Fifteen

"To be or not to be, that is the question." Allison was standing on a chair in the Gordon living room. Her friend Pamela and two boys who Sarah didn't know were sitting on the floor. "Whether 'tis nobler to suffer the outrageous arrows and things or get harmed in a sea of troubles..."

Allison bowed and her small audience clapped wildly.

"What do you think?" Pamela had an oval face and big eyes that Sarah knew would be gorgeous one day.

"I think she could do a little better remembering the words," Sarah said. "But it wasn't bad."

"I think acting is in my genes," Allison said, hopping from the chair.

"From Miss Essie, right?" Sarah gathered up what was left of the grapes on the table.

"Probably," Allison said. "I think you inherited Dad's love of schoolwork."

"Thanks." Sarah suppressed a smile as the other youthful faces in the room registered instant disapproval that *anyone* would have a love of schoolwork.

Upstairs in her room Sarah put her books on her dresser and picked up her phone. She'd known Dave all her life and there had been times when she could tell him anything, but lately even just joking around had been difficult. She dialed the familiar number, hung up, and thought about what she would say. Then she picked up the phone again and dialed as quickly as she could. Whatever came out would have to do.

"Hello?"

"Hi, you want to take me out?" she blurted the words out.

"I'd have to get my wife's permission but maybe we can arrange something." Dave Hunter's father was chuckling.

"Oh, no!" Sarah put her hand over her mouth.

"Did you want to speak to Dave?" Mr. Hunter asked.

"Yes, but don't tell him what I said," Sarah said. "Okay?"

"Fine, Sarah."

Sarah could have died from embarrassment. She

turned on the radio. An FM station came on playing a soft love song. She switched stations. She didn't want Dave to think she was trying to seduce him.

"Hello." Dave's voice was calm and quiet.

"Hi, it's Sarah."

"Oh," he said. After a pause he added, "Hi."

"Dave, I've missed just talking to you. It seems it's never the right time or something."

"Or something," he repeated. "What's up?"

"Things seem to be getting complicated in my life," Sarah said. "You've been my good friend all my life and now we can't even talk together."

"We're talking now," Dave said.

"I know," Sarah said. "Look, I want to ask you something. Okay?"

"Yeah?"

"Can...can we go out sometime, just the two of us?" She held her breath.

"I thought you were interested in...someone else." Dave didn't mention Roy's name but they both knew that was who the someone was.

"Not really," Sarah said.

"You sure could have fooled me," Dave answered.

"Well, it just...happened," Sarah said.

"Why? I don't understand."

"Look." Sarah could feel her throat tightening. "I called to ask if we could go out sometime. If you want to say no, just say so. Don't leave me hanging here. Okay?"

"Yeah, sure," Dave answered. "Look, you know I want to go out with you. Your call is just a surprise. I've got practice tomorrow till eight or nine. But then there's—"

"Wait a minute," Sarah interrupted. "How about Sunday? In the afternoon?"

"Sure, that's cool."

"Good. I'll see you then. Call me Saturday night. Okay?" Sarah smiled as if he could see over the phone.

"Okay. Yeah, okay." He sounded happy and that made Sarah giggle.

"See you in school."

When Dave hung up Sarah switched the radio back to the music station. There was another love song playing and she turned it down until she could barely hear it. She closed her eyes and thought about what Dave had said. "You know I want to go out with you," he had said. She imagined herself answering him. "Yes, darling," she imagined herself saying. "I know you want to go out with me."

Somewhere between her fifth and sixth response to Dave she fell asleep.

Tasha turned up Sarah's radio full blast and was sitting on the end of the bed doing something to her hair.

"Good grief!" Sarah forced her eyes open. "What time is it? Are we late?" She looked at her clock and saw that it was nearly seven in the morning.

"Nope, I've got an idea that's going to solve the problem with the auction. It came to me in a flash!" Tasha snapped her fingers to show how quickly the idea had come to her.

"Okay, run it by me," Sarah said. "And what are you doing to your hair?"

"Feathers," Tasha answered. "I'm wearing feathers today."

"Oh, yes, sure."

"So what kind of a girl is this Kiki?" Tasha asked. "You like her."

"Yes." Sarah rubbed her eyes and squinted to see how Tasha was arranging feathers in her hair. It looked terrible.

"Well, I was talking to Uncle Donald last night and he was saying that the one guy on the school board that Mr. Parrish couldn't influence was some guy named Grimsby," Tasha said. "You know him?"

"No," Sarah answered. "I mean I know who he is and everything. He owns a garage downtown. A big, rough guy."

"Okay, so let's you and me and Kiki go down and talk to him," Tasha said. "If we can get him to support the auction then at least we'll have somebody on our side."

"That's your bright idea?"

"You don't like it?" Tasha stopped fooling with the feathers and looked at Sarah.

"Well, it's something," Sarah said. "But why did you ask about Kiki?"

"Because you're likable, everybody knows I'm adorable, and if Kiki's all right how can he not say yes?"

"How come I'm just *likable*?" Sarah asked.

"I don't know, but you're getting more likable every day," Tasha said. "Let's get Kiki and march down to the garage after school."

"I'll call to make sure he's going to be there," Sarah said.

"Girl, how did you ever get to be so organized?" Tasha asked.

"I don't know," Sarah said. "Can I ask you something?"

"Go ahead."

"Are those feathers a fashion statement?"

"More of a fashion scream than a statement," Tasha said, laughing. "And you're going to be late for school."

Sarah shook her head as Tasha bounded out of her room and down the stairs. She was so glad that things had worked out between them.

Quick footsteps up the stairs signaled that Allison was coming. Sarah grabbed her robe and swung her legs off the bed, determined to beat her little sister to the bathroom. But Allison reached the landing first and stuck her head in Sarah's door.

"Did you see Tasha's feathers?" she asked. "Aren't they cool?"

"Wonderful," Sarah said. "Just wonderful."

Sixteen

Half of Grimsby's garage was used for all-day parking in the downtown area and the rest of it was used for repair work. The noise in the repair area was nearly overwhelming and Sarah winced as she entered.

"Hi, what can I do for you?" A sandy-haired mechanic wiped his hands on a rag.

"We have an appointment with Mr. Grimsby," Tasha said.

"He's in the back—in the office behind the pickup," the mechanic said, obviously curious about why the girls were there. "You want to be careful when you go around Mike over there."

They looked where he pointed and saw another

126

mechanic welding something to a truck body. The three girls started toward the back.

"Men love to bang on stuff," Kiki said.

"It's got something to do with evolution," Tasha shouted over the clanging. "Men are basically against it."

Philip Grimsby sat behind a battered green desk, his rounded shoulders hunched forward and his hands covered with grease. In the middle of the desk was a disassembled alternator.

"Three of you!" He nodded toward a bench. "I only have two cups for coffee."

"I don't want coffee," Sarah said.

"Me, either," Kiki made a face. "I can't stand coffee."

"That's right. I forget that kids don't like coffee. Me, I love a nice pot of coffee in the afternoon. I should do a commercial."

"I go to Hamilton High," Kiki said. "My friends here go to Murphy but they're helping us raise some money to buy video equipment."

"You want a donation?" Mr. Grimsby asked.

"They're auctioning off their services," Tasha said. "We want people to hire them for jobs. Then they can raise the money to get the video stuff."

"Wait a minute." Mr. Grimsby leaned back in his chair. "Didn't I hear something bad about that auction? Somebody called me the other day—"

"Mr. Parrish?" Sarah asked.

"No, somebody else," Mr. Grimsby said. "But

Parrish had talked to him. Said something about some kids getting into trouble."

"It was a bad rap," Kiki said. "Somebody thought this kid Steve stole a car and he didn't. He was tuning up this lady's car and he just drove it to the corner to see if it was okay and a cop stopped him."

"The lady press charges?" Grimsby asked.

"No, she told the cop the same thing that Steve did," Kiki said.

"So how did the kid get into trouble?" Mr. Grimsby's voice was full of disbelief.

"He didn't have a license," Tasha said.

"You guys sure you don't want coffee?" Mr. Grimsby asked again.

The girls said no and watched as Mr. Grimsby set up the electric pot and plugged it into the outlet over the desk. There were cups on an old black safe and he took one and wiped it out with a paper towel.

"We're selling services to businesses like yours," Sarah said. "We've got lots of capable kids willing to work hard."

"They're willing and some of them are really good with cars," Kiki added.

"So?" Mr. Grimsby sat down again in the old swivel chair.

"So, if you'd be willing to provide the opportunity to work we'll provide the worker for a few hours on a weekday or all day on Saturday, October third," Tasha said.

"You see this alternator?" Mr. Grimsby held up

the part. "Wouldn't you think they could make an alternator that wouldn't go bad? I took this one apart to see how it was made. You know what they do? They use cheap parts. Half the cars they make today are junk."

"I know what you mean," Tasha said.

"You drive?" Mr. Grimsby asked.

"Not exactly," Tasha said.

"Not exactly like this kid who did the tuneup, right?" Mr. Grimsby said.

Tasha nodded.

The coffee started to perk and the smell filled the small office.

"Hamilton's our school for kids with special needs..." Mr. Grimsby said and paused.

"Yeah." There was a hard edge to Kiki's voice as she answered Mr. Grimsby, and Sarah thought things were going badly for them.

"A lot of them just need a little special help or they have a family problem," Sarah began.

"I know a kid who went there. Didn't give a hoot about school. More interested in souping up an old Buick his uncle gave him. Kept that thing running for years. It'd still be running if they hadn't changed the emission laws." Mr. Grimsby took off the baseball cap and ran his hand over what was left of his blond hair and started to chuckle. "Guess he turned out all right, though."

"You?" Sarah asked.

"They called it the Vocational High School then.

For kids who weren't interested in going to college. A lot of guys, no girls then, did real well from my class. Some were plumbers, some were painters or repairmen. Some even went on to college and did okay." Mr. Grimsby shut off the coffeepot. "Let me do some thinking about it. I'll see what I can come up with."

"I think—" Tasha started.

"Fine!" Sarah cut off her cousin. "We appreciate your support."

Sarah offered her hand for Mr. Grimsby to shake and smiled as he put up both of his greasy hands for her to see.

"Listen, have you tried Pete Trainor down at the LunchMart? He's always looking for someone to deliver take-out meals," Mr. Grimsby said as the girls started to leave. "He's a good guy. Went to Vocational, too."

"Then he's our next stop," Sarah said.

"You wouldn't believe all the people who have businesses in Madison who were from Hamilton or schools just like them," Sarah said to her mother as she washed her hands in the sink.

"I wish you had called to tell us you'd be late from school." Mrs. Gordon passed a bowl of broccoli to Allison. "Kiki, call your mother and see if you can stay for dinner. Mr. Gordon will drive you home after we finish."

"Thank you, Mrs. G., but I think I'll just get on

home." Kiki started for the door.

"You don't have to stay but you do have to call," Mr. Gordon said.

"Okay." Kiki went to the phone in the den.

"I'm sorry." Sarah took her seat. "We just got so involved with the auction. There may be a lot of folks in Madison who are nervous about having Hamilton kids around but there are a lot that really want to help. This looks like it can really work."

"I think it's going really well," Tasha added.

"It's going to help Steve a lot, personally," Mr. Gordon said. "His father got pretty uptight about him getting picked up by the police. I think that family's a little troubled."

"Is it on officially, Donald?" Mrs. Gordon asked her husband.

"We still have to get the school board to agree to this project," Mr. Gordon said. "Mr. Parrish has been calling around and it's the school board whose opinion really counts. And I think we should get that straight before we go on," Mr. Gordon said.

"My mom says I can stay for dinner," Kiki said as she pulled up a chair to the table. "She also said not to eat too much, keep my elbows off the table, and help with the dishes."

"Did she tell you to eat your green vegetables?" Mrs. Gordon asked.

"She forgot that one, Mrs. G." Kiki smiled.

Sarah felt good about Kiki's smile. She started to think about how good she was feeling about everything and had to be asked twice to pass the bread.

"Mom, do you think I could drop out of school and become a child star?" Allison asked.

"Depends," Mrs. Gordon said. "On whether or not you eat your broccoli."

Seventeen

Sarah had convinced herself that going out with Dave was no big thing. It had helped when he had called earlier Sunday morning to tell her that the basketball coach from Providence had written him a letter.

"What did he say?" she asked.

"He said he saw me playing against Silver Lake," Dave said. "Said he liked the way I played team ball and wondered if I had considered what college I wanted to go to."

"What did you say?"

"I told him I was thinking about Providence," Dave said.

He was excited on the phone, and she imagined

him smiling. She was glad for him. His father's home repair business wasn't doing that well, and he could use any scholarship help he could get.

Things had gone well during the morning. Allison had kidded her about going out with boys, and Miss Essie had told them about her first "beau." He had come to pick her up after church and her father told him if he didn't have her back in time for evening services he was going to come looking for him with his shotgun.

Sarah wore one of Tasha's blouses and a clingy black skirt that fit her perfectly. Her new shoes didn't fit as well as they had in the store but they looked too good not to wear.

"Spray some of this behind your ears, and put some behind your knees," Tasha said, offering Sarah her cologne.

"He's not going to be sniffing behind my legs, Tasha," Sarah said, fastening her charm bracelet. "And this is only a date, not some big thing."

"Let's see your eyes." Tasha lifted Sarah's chin. "Looking good, mama."

"Thanks," Sarah said.

The doorbell rang downstairs and a moment later Allison was calling Sarah.

"Dave's here, and he's wearing a suit!" she shouted.

"Get it on, basketball star!" Sarah said when she saw Dave.

Dave didn't talk much on the way to State Park.

Sarah wondered if he was thinking about what the coach from Providence had said in the letter. There was a free indoor concert at the park's theater and they watched it for a while. A loud heavy-metal group was featured and Sarah didn't think much of it.

"Why does every heavy-metal group have one guy with his shirt off running across the stage hollering something you can't understand?" Sarah asked.

"I don't know." Dave shrugged.

"You seem far away," she said.

"You know, what I thought we would do is to row. I forgot that they only rent boats in the summer. You want to watch the people ice skating for a while? I really don't want to go to a movie."

"That what you want to do?"

"Yeah," Dave nodded. "Maybe later we can have some dinner or something."

They reached the skating rink and found a table looking down on the ice. Dave went to buy two hot chocolates and came back.

"There's one girl down there who's really good," Sarah said. "She does moves like you see on television."

Dave watched the girl skate a short distance, dip slightly, and come up in a graceful, arched back pirouette.

"She's got some strong-looking legs," he said.

"You're supposed to be impressed with her skating form, not her legs," Sarah said.

135

Dave looked down at the skaters for a while, then sipped his chocolate.

"Is there a problem?" Sarah asked.

"Like what?"

"Like why aren't you talking?"

"What do you want me to say?"

Sarah shrugged and looked away. At first she told herself that she didn't know why Dave went out with her if he wasn't happy about it. Then she remembered that she had asked him and began to feel miserable. She wondered if she should tell him she was getting a headache. That would give them both a chance to get out of the "date." On the other hand, he might think she was brushing him off.

She watched the girl skating again. The girl had long dark hair and Dave was right about her legs—they looked powerful even though they weren't too big. Even from where they sat she could see the outlines of the muscles under the white leotard.

"I like you a lot," Dave said suddenly.

"That's nice," Sarah said.

Dave nodded. He made a gesture with one hand as if he was going to say something else, then stopped.

Two kids were skating along the sides of the rink. They kept falling. First one would fall and then the other would fall and they would both laugh.

The sun was shining but it was getting cool.

"You know," Dave started again, "when I was thinking about going out with you I was trying to figure out what we were going to do. You know, a movie or something. I don't dig movies that much."

"Neither do I," Sarah said.

"Then I tried to figure out what to say to you and I couldn't figure out what to say."

The two kids who had been falling were now holding hands and skating around in a circle. They weren't bad. Sarah looked over at Dave and he was looking down at his hot chocolate. She had never thought about boys not knowing what to say. What Roy had said was just a lot of garbage, stuff that was supposed to be sexy that she didn't want to hear.

"Say you're glad to be with me," Sarah said.

Dave smiled. "I'm real glad to be with you," he said. The sincerity in his voice made her look away.

"Say I look nice," she said, not looking up at him.

"You look fantastic," he said. "But you always look fantastic."

"Say you like me," Sarah said.

"I like you," Dave said.

"Do you mean it?" Sarah asked. "Or are you just saying it because I told you to?"

"I think I mean it...hey, you know I like you."

"You're always saying what I know," Sarah said. "You said I knew you wanted to go out with me. But you never asked me."

"I didn't know if you...I don't know."

"You didn't say you liked me very convincingly," Sarah said.

"Yo, I really like you a lot," Dave said.

"How much?"

"How much?"

"Yeah, how much?" Sarah asked.

"Enough to get mad as anything about you going out with Roy," Dave said. "That was the first time I realized how much I cared for you. I was sort of thinking you were my girl and everything—"

"Without saying anything?"

"Yeah, I guess so," Dave said.

"You've got some nerve." Sarah was smiling. "Not only do you 'think I'm your girl' without saying anything to me but you bring me out to this park and let me get cold."

"You want to go get some lunch?" Dave asked.

"Maybe you can put your coat around me to warm me up," Sarah said.

Dave pulled his chair next to Sarah's and put his arm around her. He gave her a squeeze and took her hand in his.

"Now that you've had some practice you can tell me how much you like me again," she said.

Dave whispered into Sarah's ear that he cared for her a lot, more than any other girl he had ever met. He said it didn't hurt that she was beautiful.

"And you know the nicest thing about you?"

"What?" she asked, snuggling into his chest.

"Whenever I dream I have you to dream about," he said.

"Oh, Dave..." Now Sarah didn't know what to say.

When he touched her cheek she took a deep

breath. He kissed her slowly, making her feel better than she had ever felt before.

"You okay?" he asked, when he had moved away from her. "I didn't think you'd be crying."

"Me, either," she said, smiling through her tears of happiness. "Isn't it great?"

"Then..." Sarah was in her pajamas telling Tasha and Allison about her date with Dave. "I was talking and I just could not shut up. I was talking on the way to lunch. I talked all the way through lunch. I didn't give him a chance to open his mouth again. I just couldn't shut up!"

"Sounds like love to me," Tasha said.

"Sounds yucky to me," Allison said. "Dave's father has a mustache. If he grows a mustache then you'll have to kiss it."

"A fate worse than death!" Tasha said, laughing.

Eighteen

Some of the jobs were going to be done during the following week but it was still called The Big Auction Weekend. It was Cindy's idea to set up a booth on South Street, in the heart of the business district. Kiki Jones was in charge of the booth and Sarah, Tasha, and April were to be assistants.

"Everybody's excited about it, Uncle Donald," Tasha said. "And it really helped when the *Journal* did that story. But—and this is a loud and angry but—just how did Mr. Parrish get his name on this project."

"You sent the reporter from the *Journal* to me," Mr. Gordon said. "Why?"

"Because you carry more weight than we do,"

Sarah said. She was bundling the yellow pads to record the day's transactions.

"Right, and Mr. Parrish carries more weight than I do," Mr. Gordon said.

"But it's not fair if he was against it and we're doing all the work," Allison said.

"I don't see you doing any work," Sarah said.

"I'm making myself available in case you guys need fresh ideas," Allison said.

"Wonderful," Sarah said. "But Allison's right, it isn't fair. It looks like he was the driving force behind this whole program."

"You girls were wonderful," Mr. Gordon said. "Your idea of going to Mr. Grimsby was good, and the work you put into reaching other people was excellent. But what we were looking for is the equipment for the program at Hamilton. The best way of getting that is by letting Mr. Parrish get as much credit as possible. That way he becomes supportive instead of being against us."

"My father used to say that the only thing that was fair was that both teams had a chance to show up at the same time," Tasha said. "After that it was kick, scratch, and scuffle and then look at the scoreboard to see who won."

"That certainly sounds like my brother," Mr. Gordon said. "Now, do you need a lift downtown?"

"Are you trying to tell us that it's time to go to work, Dad?" Sarah asked.

There were nearly a hundred kids from Hamilton

and fifteen kids from Murphy gathered at the Village Green. Shoppers stopped by and asked what they were doing and some of them offered jobs on the spot.

"The funniest thing," Kiki said, "is that so many people just want to give donations. When we were looking for donations before nobody wanted to offer anything."

"What I need to find out," Steve said, "is don't any of these people have kids?"

"What's that mean?" Tasha asked.

"Mostly they want people to clean their yards, pick up leaves, and bundle up papers. How come they don't just get their kids to do that kind of thing?"

"Hey, Steve." A thin kid wearing an Oakland Raiders jacket put his hand on Steve's shoulder. "I just cleaned up your yard. Your father gave ten dollars for me to pick up the leaves and all those flyers people throw into your yard."

"My father hired you?"

"Not only that," the thin kid said, "but he said that he's been after you to do it for three weeks."

"I was just going to get around to it." Steve grinned.

A man from the mayor's office came over and spoke to Mr. Gordon, telling him that he wanted him to make sure that the kids didn't clutter up the Village Green and that they left it clean. Mr. Gordon asked Steve to be in charge of a cleanup detail. Steve got paper bags from the guy from the mayor's office and started out.

"Steve's a good kid," Mr. Gordon said. "One of the best in the school. All he needs is a chance to prove himself."

The rest of the day went well. At the end of the day Kiki turned over the money they had earned to Mr. Gordon, and Mr. Gordon, in turn, found Mr. Parrish and turned the money over to him.

"Good job, kids." Mr. Parrish was smiling and shaking every available hand. "Good job."

"The earnings from The Big Auction Weekend total two thousand forty-eight dollars and seventeen cents," Sarah announced.

"How did we get seventeen cents?" Kiki asked.

Nobody knew how they got the seventeen cents but everybody was happy. By the time Sarah and Tasha got home they were exhausted, but not as exhausted as April. She was crying when she showed up.

"What happened?" Mrs. Gordon asked. "Are you all right?"

"Oh, sure, I'm all right now," April said. "But you should have seen me before. I decided to volunteer my services. So I'm sitting on the Green with everybody else and this woman comes over to me and asks me if I'll walk her dog. She's carrying this little dog in her arms. I say okay and she says for me to come with her. She takes me to a car and there's another dog in the car."

143

"A Great Dane!" Allison said.

"No, a terrier," April said. "Anyway, she wants me to walk the dog while she goes shopping. She wants me to be back at the car in forty minutes.

"So I'm walking this dog down South Street and he's pulling at the leash. Then he gets away and starts running and I'm running after him. Well, that dog ran fifteen blocks before he stopped. I'm yelling at people to get him, I'm screaming at the dog, I'm going crazy. Finally he runs all the way back to Speedwell Avenue and I catch him near the drugstore. Then I take him back to the car and this lady is waiting there and she wants to know where I've been. So I said I was just walking around and she tells me she was afraid that I had kidnapped her dumb dog."

"How much did you earn?" Tasha asked.

"Two dollars."

"Then you done good," Tasha said.

"First money I ever earned in my life," April said. "I was pretty proud of it."

"And I'm pretty proud of all of you," Mr. Gordon said.

"You're okay, too, Mr. Gordon," April said. "If you ever need another daughter, give me a call."

"You're on the top of my list," Mr. Gordon said.

PINE

Nineteen

"Okay, this is it. I've just solved the major problem in all our lives," Kwame said as he sat down at the center table at 18 Pine. April was right behind him carrying a huge pizza. Cindy, Jennifer, Sarah, and Tasha were just finishing the one they had ordered fifteen minutes earlier.

April elbowed Kwame's arm out of the way and sat down on the last available chair. "If anybody's solved our problems, it's me."

"So what is our major problem?" Tasha asked.

"Money!" Kwame said. "Making a living. That's why you go to college, right? That's why you make up résumés and go job hunting. What I've decided—"

"What we've decided," April interrupted, "was that we should each have a major fund-raiser. So, say the first year we have a fund-raiser for me. Only we plan the whole thing so we make a lot of money like they do on television."

"So we raise nine million dollars for April," Kwame said. "Then she's set for life. And she doesn't even need nine million. We'll give her three million and that leaves six million for the rest of us. A million for me, one for Jennifer, one for Cindy, and one for Tasha and Sarah. That leaves two million to advertise the next fund-raiser."

"Wait, let's check this out." Tasha pulled out a slice of pizza. "Me and Sarah only get one million to share between us?"

"That's because you're related," Kwame said. "And also because Sarah, who was the love of my life, has now become an item with Dave Hunter."

"And you've just written me off completely?" Jennifer said. "And all this time I've been saving myself just for your arms."

"Let's skip the small talk," Kwame said. "Is our idea brilliant or what?"

"There's got to be a catch here somewhere," Tasha said. "I mean, if this is such a good idea why doesn't everybody do it?"

" ...do you know a lot of people don't do it?"

" ...never hear about it," Sarah said.

" ...money that way would you go

around advertising it?" April asked.

"Girl, you've been hanging around Kwame too long," Sarah said. "You apparently don't know about his condition. He's got Mozzarella Mind. That's what happens when the cheese from all these pizzas starts to clog up the little neurons that connect the different parts of your brain. We'll all get it sooner or later but Kwame's got it now."

"Here come Steve and José," Tasha said. "Hide the pizza."

"You can't hide a pie this big," April said. "But don't mention the fund-raiser."

"Come on over guys. We've got a get-rich-quick plan," Sarah called.

"You got two dollars?" José asked. "I got to get home."

Jennifer had two dollars to lend him and made him sign an IOU. "Could you sign it in blood?" she asked.

"You got no heart, woman," José said.

"I've got to get home, too," Tasha said. "This absolutely wonderful boy said that he adored my guitar playing and I just have to practice before he hears me again. I think I'm his personal muse."

"I'm out of here, too," Sarah said. "April, do call me when you and Kwame decide when it's my turn to get a million."

"Turn away from these millions if you want," Kwame called after the Gordons. "But when I'm filthy rich don't come crawling to me for pizza money!"

PINE

Twenty

Outside 18 Pine St. a light rain was falling. Sarah took Tasha's arm and the cousins leaned forward into the wind as they headed for the bus stop.

"So who's this boy?" Sarah asked.

"I don't like him all that much," Tasha said. "I think he likes me, though. But who can blame him? I mean, he is young."

"I know what you mean," Sarah said. "These young boys do go on, don't they? And they're so excitable!"

"Well, I certainly did think that was one of Dave's nicer attributes," Tasha said.

"Dave excites me because he's in love with me," Sarah said. "He thinks he just likes me a lot but the

148

boy is stone in love with me. He adores the ground I walk on."

"You love him?" Tasha asked.

"Yeah, I think so," Sarah said. "I know I'm going to be in love with him for the rest of the week, at least," she added with a laugh.

Sarah and Tasha reached the bus stop just as the Number 81 bus came along, and they got on.

"What do you think of Kwame's plan?" Sarah asked.

"I hope he gets it to work," Tasha answered. "Hey, I got something else to say. You want to hear something heavy?"

Sarah looked at Tasha to see if she was being serious, and saw that her cousin had tears in her eyes. She put her hand on Tasha's and searched for words. "I'm ready for anything you have to say," Sarah said.

"Look, cousin, I'm glad to be going where we're going," Tasha said.

"Where's that?" Sarah asked.

"Home," Tasha said. "It feels good saying it, and it feels good doing it."

Sarah looked away, the tears stinging her eyes. Emotions ran through her. She remembered how jealous she had been of Tasha, and how angry she had been. Now she felt ashamed of those feelings.

"Tasha..." she started.

"Oh, shut up, girl!"

"Yeah," Sarah said. "I know what you mean."

Coming in Book 2, The Party

"Tasha is kissing a boy outside!" Allison whispered, and pointed toward the window.

"Then that is none of your business," Sarah said. "And if you snoop I'll tell Daddy."

"Tattletale!" Allison pouted and beat a hasty retreat for her own room.

Sarah made sure her door was closed, turned her lights off, and went to the window. Carefully she pulled down one slat of the venetian blinds. There, in the semidarkness below her window, was a figure standing near the gate. It looked like one rather heavy person until Tasha disengaged herself from Dave Hunter's arms.

Jennifer's throwing a party for the hottest rap group in town, and Tasha is messing with Dave. Don't miss a thing—just head downtown to 18 Pine St.